Spirited Sisters

Smooth Operator
&
Hunting Spirits

Lynn Emery

Ghosts & goblins giving you the blues?
Call 1-800-Spirits

Note:
Vampires, werewolves, and trolls
require special rates

Smooth Operator

1.

On a sunny Thursday afternoon in June, Charmaine sat across from her newest "client" and stared back at her. A small air conditioner worked to keep the humid New Orleans heat at bay. All the bad vibes from this woman made Charmaine feel claustrophobic, as though her usually pleasant home office was stuffed with greasy smog. From the top of her flaming red hair to the tips of her gaudy rhinestone encrusted acrylic fingernails, Kiesha Front screamed "gold digger".

Keisha got up and started making a circle of the room examining the decor. She started by reading framed degrees and certifications on the wall. Charmaine proudly displayed her diplomas. She loved being a therapist with a little something extra, psychic ability. Her gift of sight gave her a rare insight into her clients. She'd had terrific success helping them find the source of their pain and recover. Others she'd helped avoid dangers creeping toward them from the past. Despite her attempts to keep that part of her practice discreet, the word got out.

For the past year most who came to her wanted more of the supernatural help than therapy. Most couldn't pay much. Charmaine's professional reputation among her more conventional colleagues had suffered. Referrals from local psychiatrists and other counselors dried up. Three insurance companies removed her from their provider networks. Charmaine had had to supplement her income with part-time jobs for the past two years, including a stint working at a local dollar store. And now this.

"Impressive credentials," Keisha said as she leaned closer to stare at one document. "You've re-invented yourself since we were kids in the projects."

"So have you I see," Charmaine said in a dry tone. She remembered Kiesha from high school, though she'd been a year behind Charmaine. Keisha had always been determined to get attention and get ahead.

Keisha gave a short laugh. "Yeah, you could say that." Then she turned and read out loud from another framed document. "So you're a 'Certified Clinical Hypnotherapist'. Bet that comes in handy."

"It does at times," Charmaine replied.

"Don't think you can try it on me. I'm resistant to that kinda mess," Keisha said, tossing the words over her shoulder without looking at Charmaine.

"Would you like a glass of sweet tea?" Charmaine asked.

"See, that's what I mean. You start off with a simple request. Nothing important, but you establish a connection and start a chain of me doing what you suggest." Keisha came to a decorative mirror on another wall. She gazed at her make-up, patted her hair and turned to Charmaine. "No, I don't want tea. Can't stand the stuff."

"I offer everyone some form of refreshment. Maybe you'd like..."

"I'm fine, Ms. Joliet. Hmm, that sounds too formal. I'll call you Charmaine," Keisha said and smiled. "Nice how you turned this addition your mama used as a beauty shop into your office."

Charmaine smiled back at her. "Thank you. And of course you can call me Charmaine. You're right. No need for formality."

Keisha raised an eyebrow. She strolled back to the chair facing Charmaine's desk, sat down and crossed her shapely brown legs. "You're good, but it still won't work. Look, I've done my homework on you. I have... friends who specialized in... Let's just call it research."

"Research, right." Charmaine folded her arms.

"Okay, don't get an attitude. This proposal can do good things for both of us," Keisha said. She sighed and uncrossed her legs. "My husband has a lot of money. He's as mean as a bucket of rattlesnakes, and he has lots of enemies. You need money, and you have skills and experience in making a man... disappear. I'll keep your secret, pay you money and you'll have something on me."

"So we'll both have to keep our mouths shut," Charmaine added and clenched her teeth.

"Exactly." Keisha nodded with satisfaction.

"Why shouldn't I just go to the police? You don't have proof that I made anyone 'disappear' as you put it. Or I could go to your hubby and tell him of your sincere desire to get rid of him," Charmaine shot back.

Keisha's expression hardened. "You don't really want to put your dear, emotionally fragile baby sister through the stress. She's had a few issues since that ugly incident back when you were kids, hasn't she? Poor little Jessica. In the past two years alone she's been arrested twice for soliciting, three times for possession of weed, three times for assaulting her male customers. One might even wonder if she's about to become a female serial killer. Girlfriend has some serious anger issues."

Every hair on Charmaine's body stood at attention. A prickle of fear mixed with loathing shot through her. "Don't threaten my sister."

"We don't have to be enemies. You two had it hard growing up. I've been there, girl. I'm like you, Charmaine; a survivor. I learned to use men for what I want, instead always being used by them," Keisha said with a grimace.

"No, you're not like me. And you're damn sure not going to be my friend coming in here trying to blackmail me into killing your rich husband," Charmaine hissed.

Kiesha stood and looped her expensive gold metallic leather purse over the crook of once arm. She actually almost looked elegant, minus the hair and fingernails. "Jessica is in trouble again. She's going to need a good lawyer."

"What the hell are you talking about?" Charmaine gripped the imitation leather covering the arms of her cheap office chair.

"Call her hooker pal Diamond if you don't believe me. You haven't talked to Jessica in three days. That's because she's in the Orleans Parish lock-up, sweetie. She knifed a guy over drugs or something." Keisha picked up a small note pad from Charmaine's desk. She wrote down a phone number and held out the pad. When Charmaine didn't take it, Keisha tossed it onto the desk. "Call me when you're ready to talk."

"You're lying," Charmaine said trying not to panic. Dread washed over her like bone chilling water on her skin.

"You already know I'm not. Go help your sister. I can give you the bail money as part of your payment. We both know she won't do well in a jail cell," Keisha replied. She put on designer sunglasses and walked out.

Shaking, Charmaine went to the office door leading to the outside and slammed home both deadbolts. She went back to her phone to call the parish jail. Then she stopped and put down the cordless handset. Charmaine's second sight, the gift that was both a blessing and a curse told her that Keisha, aka Mrs. James LeLand Front, had not lied. Jessi needed to be rescued. Again.

2.

Club Mellow lived up to its name and then some. No loud music or rowdy patrons allowed. Saturday night at seven thirty Charmaine sat in a booth with seats upholstered in real leather the color of red wine. She was drinking whiskey. Her good friend Scotty stood behind the bar. Scotty, Jessi and Charmaine; they'd been family for over fifteen years. Their bond had been forged on the street, three homeless kids living hard to escape hell at home. When he turned eighteen Scotty joined the Army. He'd been Special Forces, skills he brought back to the street after serving for six years.

Despite being the owner of the club and three other thriving businesses in Orleans Parish, Scotty still liked playing bartender from time to time. At six feet four and with muscles all over, he could also be the bouncer. One of several professions he'd had in his murky past. But his formidable presence wasn't the reason Club Mellow was so peaceful. The clientele kept it that way. They needed a discreet safe harbor to meet like-minded people. Upscale hook-ups is how Jessi sarcastically described it. Singles and couples retreated to the softly light elegant club to live out their fantasies.

Charmaine came to ease the sexual tension that gnawed at her when she felt threatened, lonely or stressed. A psychologist had helped Charmaine understand that her hyper-sexuality resulted from years of sexual abuse. She and Jessica had suffered at the hands of their two successive step-fathers. They'd come to associate sex with all emotions.

For Jessi, sex became a means to an end; a way to be in control. Of course the sense of control wasn't real. It only lasted the few hours she spent servicing her clients; tying up men or women, ordering them to surrender to Jessi's every whim until they screamed in ecstasy. Then she plunged back into a dark place that only drugs could banish.

All this insight came from six years of therapy for Charmaine. Dr. Lance told her that one day she'd accept true intimacy and love, and then she wouldn't need Club Mellow. Charmaine knew differently. Unlike Jessi, Charmaine loved sex. The physical pleasure of being with someone as an adult and by her own choosing was Charmaine's drug. Charmaine didn't have all of the answers. She didn't need them. Her life worked for her. Mostly.

Scotty strolled over to Charmaine's booth after his employee, the real bartender, took over. He held two short tumblers with dark gold liquid in each hand. He plunked one down on the table in front of Charmaine's almost empty glass. Then he eased his tall frame onto the leather seat across from her, took a swig from his own tumbler and sighed.

"Hello Charming Charmaine," Scotty rumbled in his basso voice and winked at her.

She finished off the last bit of whiskey in one tumbler and picked up the full one. "Beam me up, Scotty." Charmaine took a sip and let the whiskey tickle down the back of her throat.

"Jim Beam," Scotty said completing the old joke they shared.

They shared a companionable silence for another ten minutes, watching couples and some threesomes get acquainted. Everyone chatted as though they were just out with friends. Soft laughter and conversation floated around the room. Smooth jazz mixed with R&B tunes played over the sound system. Through an archway was another room with a dance floor and a stage raised a foot higher. The regular Saturday night band would start to play at nine o'clock. Scotty and Charmaine exchanged a few sentences of small talk the way southerners did before getting down to business.

"So was I right?" Charmaine asked and studied Scotty.

"On target. Keisha is a grifter, a con artist who hit it big time when she married James LeLand Front, an older man with money. Good money, too," Scotty said. He raised his glass in a mock salute. "Go on with yo bad self, Miss K."

"How good?" Charmaine asked.

"He sold his packaging business in 1983 for a cool ten million to a Fortune 500 company. At thirty-five he was too young to just put his feet up. Dude started a high tech company three years later. Four years later he sold that company for one hundred million. Set his four kids up and did consulting. He had a heart attack and a stroke in 2006. Divorced his fourth wife in 2009 when he met the lovely Keisha Grant."

"I knew from the way she talked to me that first day that Keisha had been in the game. She summed up the ways of a player and jail house philosophy without missing a beat," Charmaine replied.

Scotty nodded. "She's served time, but I see you figured that one out. Keisha hasn't been able to drop her ghetto so easy. She didn't blend with polite society as she'd hoped."

Charmaine snorted. "Once a hood rat, always a hood rat; at least for some."

She was about to go on when a tall, fine looking man with skin like caramel candy walked into the barroom. Her body hummed, and not just from the psychic vibes. He wore a short-sleeved olive green cotton knit top that clung to his muscled chest. Dark khaki denim slacks hugged his narrow waist and molded to his thick thighs.

"That's him, huh?" Charlene murmured, covering her comment by raising the glass to her mouth.

Scotty didn't glance at him, but kept his back to the man and his voice low. "Mr. Slick. I told him I'd point you out. Got me a fifty for doing it, too."

"You backstabber," Charmaine quipped and managed not to laugh.

"Enjoy your drink, Charmaine, and don't stay away so long next time," Scotty said in a normal volume and smiled at her.

Then Scotty moved to a table a few feet away and quietly chatted up more customers. Scotty didn't look in her direction again. He seemed very relaxed as he played the role of the good business owner. Charmaine made a mental note to suggest he take up acting. Then she switched her attention back to the man.

She guessed he was about six feet one. He sat down at the bar and pretended to finally notice Charmaine was staring at him. He took the glass the bartender put on bar in front of him and lifted it in salute to her. Charmaine matched his gesture. He got up and walked to her.

"Good evening. I..."

"Yes, you most certainly can join me," Charmaine broke in. She brushed her shoulder length hair with her fingers.

"I'm Lorenzo," he said and sat down. His gaze covered Charmaine from head to toe. "Very nice to meet you."

"Same here." Charmaine gave him an appraising glance in turn. She moistened her lips and smiled at him as though appreciating the view. "If you've been hanging out at the club lately, then Scotty is right. I have been away too long."

"Well, let's not regret the past. We're here now," Lorenzo replied smoothly. His dark eyebrows framed cocoa brown eyes perfectly. His lips curved up in a handsome smile.

Lorenzo Thomas, afro-Latino, age thirty-five; three years older than Charmaine. Scotty had filled Charmaine in on him a few days earlier. Lorenzo Thomas was a private investigator of the shady variety. Scotty had easily dug up the background on him when Charmaine asked him to track down the scoop on Keisha. But Scotty hadn't mentioned that he looked like a male supermodel and oozed sex appeal. Charmaine's libido set her body humming again. Playing with him was an added bonus. The alluring smile she flashed at Lorenzo was totally genuine.

"I agree, Lorenzo. Ahh, that name rolls off the tongue," Charmaine said softly.

"I'm half Puerto Rican," he replied and sipped more of his drink.

"And the other half?" Charmaine leaned forward as though eager to hear his every word.

"Pure Houston ninja from the Fifth Ward, baby," he replied and grinned at her. "And you?"

Charmaine shrugged. "New Orleans East."

"Alright then. I use to visit friends that way. To what NO used to be, the good and the bad," Lorenzo said and tapped her glass against hers.

"Co-sign," Charmaine said and they both took deep pulls from their drinks.

For the next two hours they exchanged small talk about their favorite hip hop artists from back in the day, movies and more. When the band started they followed the music and danced a few times. As the night grew older, the band played slower tunes. Charmaine pressed her body to Lorenzo and didn't object when his wide hands moved lower on her body. By the fourth song he gently cupped her buttocks, rubbing his hands over the soft fabric of her red leggings.

"You look damn good, Charmaine," Lorenzo breathed in her ear. "I'm in pain because of you, girl."

"Then let's make this party private. Scotty's hotel is right next door; a classy place," Charmaine whispered, her lips brushing his ear lobe. She did a bump and grind against his pelvis that made him moan.

"Let's go," he croaked.

Lorenzo swiped perspiration from his forehead and led them down a softly lit hallway leading to the hotel lobby. In a few minutes the efficient registration clerk had them checked into a room on the fourth floor. They went to the elevator, got in and immediately started kissing and groping each other. Charmaine giggled as the strong man pressed her against the wall.

"Slow down, baby. We don't want to finish up before we get started," Charmaine said.

"No worries, girl. I'm an all night man, just like that bunny with those batteries. I can keep going," Lorenzo bragged. He licked her neck and rubbed her breast roughly.

"Well alright then," Charmaine replied with enthusiasm.

The elevator bumped to a stop and the doors slid open. Another couple brushed past them into the elevator, the man with his face averted. The man didn't have to worry. Lorenzo barely noticed him. He was too intent on pulling Charmaine to Room 407. He mumbled a few curse words when they had to walk farther down the hall than he'd expected. Lorenzo shoved the key card into the lock.

"We're in the House of Pleasure, girl. Now come here." Lorenzo pulled Charmaine against his body with one long arm and shoved the door shut with the other.

"Take charge," Charmaine whispered as he lifted her from the floor.

She wrapped her legs around him and kissed him hard. Lorenzo moaned, breathing hard in between trying to pull open her top with his teeth. He let her slide to the floor and Charmaine pushed away from him. She dropped her small purse on the dresser against one wall. Then she undid the tie of the sheer cardigan she wore over a black camisole. Lorenzo pulled at his clothes without taking his gaze from Charmaine's striptease performance. She went to the night stand and hit the button on a clock radio. A thumping R&B tune poured through the compact, but excellent speakers. Then she resumed her dance. Charmaine took off her cami and leggings. She swayed to the music wearing only panties and a bra the color of Louisiana hot sauce.

"You know how to move," Lorenzo said. With quick movements he draped his clothes over the chair next to the small desk in the room. He'd stripped down and wore only silky black underwear.

Charmaine gazed at the impressive bump straining against the fabric of his briefs. "You know how to impress."

"You ain't seen nothin' yet, girl," Lorenzo growled.

"Then bring it," Charmaine replied.

In a flash his long legs brought him across the short space between them. Lorenzo yanked open the front hooks of her bra. Charmaine flinched at the rough treatment, but only briefly. She shrugged to allow the straps to fall from her shoulders as her breasts bounced free. Lorenzo groaned and sank to his knees. Charmaine cradled his head in both her hands and looked into his eyes. She murmured softly to him, a string of commands mixed in with lusty bedroom talk. Before long, the big man was under her control. He told her what she wanted to know.

After thirty minutes of questioning, Charmaine started to fill his mind with false erotic memories. Then she stepped away to examine him again.

"Since we're here and you're so awesomely equipped, why don't I see if you told the truth," Charmaine said softly. "I'm gonna have you prove you're an all-night man."

3.

The next morning Charmaine went to the housing development in New Orleans East. Built by a famous actor after the devastation of Hurricane Katrina, the houses had brought a least this part of the city back to life. Jessi's friend Diamond lived in one of the neat garden homes with her youngest kid, a two year old baby girl named Indyah. Diamond tried several times to get out of the street life, but minimum wage jobs hadn't been her style. She and Jessi were careful to keep business at a different location. Charmaine parked in the narrow driveway and got out. The cheerful pale yellow paint of the house gleamed in the sunshine. Charmaine had to step over a tiny tricycle left on the sidewalk. She rang the doorbell and Diamond answered.

Dressed in leopard print leggings and a big sweatshirt, Diamond grinned at her. "Hey you, c'mon in." She kissed Charmaine on the cheek and motioned her inside.

"How're you doin' and how is Indyah?" Charmaine said and glanced around. She dropped her purse on the coffee table. The house looked neat enough.

"I'm fine. The baby is doing great. She's with her grandmamma today." Diamond led the way into her small living room. "Jessi, well, she's gettin' better. That jail scared her. They got a lot of crazy people in there, girl. Damn, I'm glad we pulled together the money for her bail. It wasn't all her fault this time, Charmaine.

Jessi came down the stairs wearing a silky floral robe and fuzzy bunny slippers. She kissed Charmaine on the cheek and padded into the kitchen. "Don't bother

tryin' ta convince her, girl. Big sister is going to say it was my crazy ass fault no matter what you say. You want some coffee?"

Charmaine followed Jessi to the kitchen
and sat on one of two stools at the small
breakfast bar. "Yes, and I want to know if
you're okay."

"I'm fine," Jessi said, and waved a hand
without looking at Charmaine.

Despite her words, Jessi's hand shook as
she picked up two ceramic mugs. Charmaine saw the tremors. When Jessi turned
to pick up the glass coffee pot, her swollen
right cheek was visible. Charmaine swal-
lowed hard and fought the urge to rush
over to her. Jessi didn't respond well to being babied. Too many years of having to
tough out what life threw at her had made
her immune to it.

"How'd that happen to your face?"
Charmaine asked.

"Some fool started ranting and raving,
swung on me before I could react. I got
her back good though, you can believe
that." Jessi dumped three teaspoons of
sugar in her own mug and a generous

helping of real cream. She pushed the mug of hot black coffee across the counter to Charmaine.

"That place is more like a psycho ward than a jail," Diamond added. She sat on a second stool. She accepted a mug from Jessi and sipped.

"So tell me about this incident that got you arrested, Jessi." Charmaine squinted at her.

"I was working the massage house down off Carrollton. Strictly legit, Charmaine and don't roll your eyes at me," Jessi added. "Anyway, this foreign fool starts trying to negotiate. I tells him 'Bitch, this ain't the discount store and we don't run sales'. Then he gets up in my face and tries to lay his hands on me. I don't know who called the police."

"And that's another thing, Miss Susie has private security. These little disagreements gets handled on the spot, no cops." Diamond shook her head.

"Maybe his buddy that came with him got scared. Betcha one thing, that dude knows how we do business in New Orleans now." Jessi grunted and sipped coffee. She looked at Charmaine. "Let's save time. I know all your lectures by heart, so save your breath."

"No more lectures," Charmaine said. She frowned and thought about Jessi's account. Something about the details nagged at her for a few seconds before Jessi's voice broke into her thoughts.

"Look, I'm doing okay. I'm going to pay you back for the bail cause I know you ain't got disposable income to be spending on me. Besides, I got savings." Jessi pulled out a wad of bills and came around the counter.

"Don't worry about..." Charmaine shook her head.

Jessi grabbed Charmaine's purse off the coffee table and carefully stuffed the money into a pocket. She snapped it shut. "Don't flash that around."

"Jessi, I don't need your money," Charmaine said.

"Quit lyin', Char. How'd you know so quick about me being arrested anyway? I told Diamond not to call you." Jessi glanced at her friend.

"Wasn't me," Diamond said quickly.

"Never mind. Just be extra careful for the next few days, okay?" Charmaine said. "You, too, Diamond."

Jessi gazed at Charmaine for several seconds. "What's going on?"

Jessi had psychic ability like Charmaine. She heard voices. It started when she was seven. Diagnosed as schizophrenic, Jessi had been in and out of psychiatric hospitals most of her childhood. Charmaine finally figured out that Jessi could hear the dead. Those who were unsettled wanted to tell their stories. One more reason Jessi started smoking pot and doing drugs when she was thirteen, to make the voices go away. The sisters were more than close. At times they could sense, see and hear one another no matter the distance. But the connection wasn't consistent, more like a spotty cell phone signal. Silence stretched between them.

"I'll tell you later. I promise. You don't need to know right now," Charmaine replied finally.

You be careful," Jessi said and walked close to Charmaine. Her voice shook as she crossed her arms tightly against her slender body.

"Scotty is helping me," Charmaine said.

Diamond got up and stood between them, her arms on both their shoulders. The three women exchanged hugs..

4.

Five days later Keisha sat in the same chair in Charmaine's home office. But unlike the last time she wasn't alone. Lorenzo sat next to her. His gaze darted around every few minutes to check his surroundings. Keisha had changed her look. The bright red hair was now a more subdued auburn color. Her rust colored designer sleeveless dress complimented her new hair color and skin. Lorenzo wore a light gray knit cotton shirt tucked into a pair of navy blue slacks. His well shined leather loafers had to be worth at least two hundred dollars. Charmaine was wondering if

Keisha had paid for them when he cleared his throat as if to get her attention. Charmaine had allowed Keisha to do most of the talking for the last ten minutes.

"So you've had a chance to check out what I told you. Congrats on getting your sister out of jail. But she'll be back in if you don't cooperate," Keisha said in a crisp, business-like tone.

Charmaine smiled at Lorenzo, and he grinned back. "I'm a little distracted, with everything going on you understand."

"You've had a busy week," Lorenzo murmured with a smug expression.

"Hmm, yes. Action packed," Charmaine replied.

Keisha glanced at Lorenzo sharply and then back to Charmaine. "Time to quit messing around. My husband likes to play poker with his old pals at this seedy dump of a night club once a week. Make it look like he got caught up in a drive-by, an innocent bystander in the wrong place at the wrong time. Or maybe a street robbery. That's it. He was mugged a couple of years ago and he fought back. This time he's going to lose that fight. Yeah, I like that better. That's going to be very believable."

"Clever plan. Except I'm not going to do it," Charmaine said.

"You will," Keisha shot back.

Lorenzo sat forward and stared at Charmaine. "Four years ago Diamond's abusive boyfriend disappeared. He'd broken her oldest kid's arm, and beat him senseless. The kid is still a cripple. The guy only got a couple of years in jail for it. Diamond lost custody of the kid."

"We know where he is, and he ain't breathin'," Keisha snapped. "And here's something even more interesting. Your second step-father went "poof!" back in the day. His family hasn't seen or heard from him for almost sixteen years. About the same time you and your baby sister ran away from home. With her violent history I'm thinking the police will be very interested in this story, especially one Officer Deon Morehouse. He's vindictive and mean as hell, still mad at Keisha for reporting that he demanded a blow job during an arrest. She should have kept her mouth shut."

"I gotta figure out how to get that crook off the police force. But I'm not going to kill your husband. Do it yourself." Charmaine stood.

"Maybe another trip to the infamous Orleans Parish lock-up for little Jessica will convince you. I don't think she can take another overnight stay, much less a week or a month." Keisha stood as well and glared at Charmaine.

"You've told me some very colorful stories. You have no evidence, just two overactive imaginations. Go look in the woods off River Road in Chalmette near the Murphy Refinery." Charmaine watched their expressions go from smug to shock. "The body they dig up will be an older woman named Marian Durocher. She went missing and so did eighty thousand dollars from her bank account. Keisha, you worked as her caregiver but used a different name. Both her kids died years ago, and nobody cared enough to check on her. That's a real whodunit, huh?"

Keisha stumbled back and almost fell over the chair. She reached out for Lorenzo, but he'd moved back from her. "How the hell did you... Lorenzo, do something!"

Lorenzo held up both hands. "Like what?"

Charmaine wore a razor sharp smile. "So it seems we have a stand-off. No hard evidence on either of us, but enough to make life very unpleasant if the cops start asking questions."

"We'll fix you, bitch. Just wait and see." Keisha grabbed Lorenzo's arm and pulled him along behind her as she stomped out of the door.

Scotty came into the office from the hallway leading to Charmaine's house. He went to the window and watched Keisha's red BMW sedan speed off. "Is that the end?"

"I think so. Keisha is a ruthless black widow, but she's not stupid." Charmaine joined Scotty at the window. "I have another problem. Jessi has disappeared."

"She's been pulling those vanishing acts for a good long time." Scotty let go of the curtain and turned to Charmaine. "But this time something is different, huh?"

"Something's very different, and in a bad way. She's outta control, Scotty." Charmaine looked at her friend with a worried frown.

"Then we'll find her." Scotty gave Charmaine a big brother type hug.

"I have a feeling we better find her soon," she said quietly.

5.

Charmaine drove through three stop signs and narrowly missed a slow-moving car that pulled out from a driveway. She saw flashing lights from a New Orleans police cruiser behind her. Slowing down she pulled her Chevy Equinox along the curb. Her throat tightened until she gasped with the effort to swallow. When the cop car blew by her and kept going, Charmaine hissed out the breath she'd been holding. She trembled with relief that another poor sucker would get stopped this time. Then she began to shake all over. What if that cop was on the way to the same address Charmaine had?

"No time, girl. You got no time to freak out," Charmaine shouted at herself.

She gulped in three deep breaths, let them out to steady her nerves, and then drove on. Two and a half miles later she turned on the dimly lit street. The GPS on her phone chimed three times. Charmaine pulled up to the house. When she recognized Scotty's SUV, Charmaine jammed her car into park and jumped out. In seconds she walked quickly up the cement walkway to the front door. When she pressed a lighted button the bell seemed to clang way too loud. A series of clicks and snapping sounds preceded the door inching open. Then it swung wide. Scotty unlocked the storm door covering the solid wood one.

"Come on in. She's okay," he said and smoothly stepped aside to allow Charmaine in. He glanced up and down the street before shutting the door and locking it. "Go down the hall, second bedroom on the left."

Charmaine nodded and followed his directions. Jessi lay across a full-sized bed that took up most of the tiny room. Diamond sat in a stuffed chair staring at a small television with the sound on mute. She pressed a fist to her mouth when she saw Charmaine. Tears rolled down her face.

"I did it this time, Charmaine. You can't keep saving my psycho ass. I killed that dude." Jessi looked strangely calm. Her voice was steady. She stared at the bedroom wall, her eyes glassy and her expression blank.

"She's been like this since we got here. That's makin' me more crazy than if she was screaming and bouncin' off the walls," Diamond said softly and started crying, a hand over her mouth to muffle her sobs.

"You need to pull it together. We all gotta think straight. Go get you some water, or coffee, or something," Charmaine replied, sounding more composed than she felt inside.

"'Kay," Diamond said. She swiped at her face and left the bedroom.

Charmaine gazed at her sister for a few minutes. She tried to coax Jessi into talking, but got nothing. So she headed back to the living room.

Scotty murmured into the Bluetooth headset looped over his right ear. "Yeah, a quick clean up job. Right, right. Cool. Call me in one hour to check in."

"How bad is it?" Charmaine dropped her car keys into the cross-body bag she still wore.

"Keisha's husband is dead in a motel room on the West Bank. Jessi was with him. I'd followed her after getting a tip from a buddy. I bribed a motel maid and got in the room. Front was on the bed naked from the waist down with his throat cut wide open. Jessi was so high we couldn't get her to make any sense. My buddy and me moved fast and got her outta there." Scotty shook his head. "How the hell did they set that up?"

"Keisha said she'd deliver some payback. Damn!" Charmaine paced in a circle while raking fingers through her hair. "Damn!"

"I'm pretty sure we weren't followed," Scotty said. He strode to the windows and looked out once again.

Diamond came in carrying a tray with cans of soda, a tray of cheese and crackers. "Y'all might as well snack. I'm not sure we can get anything delivered in this neighborhood."

"Whose house is this?" Charmaine asked and waved away the can of soda Diamond tried to hand her.

"My cousin. She's visiting relatives in Atlanta, and I told her I'd check on the place. I've got a key. Sure you don't want something on your stomach?" Diamond said. She picked up a cube of pepper jack cheese and nibbled on it.

"No way. I'm close to puking from stress as it is," Charmaine replied and looked away from the tray.

"At least we got a few hours to take a breath and think about our next move. My other buddy went over to check out the motel," Scotty said. He was about to go on but his cell phone vibrated. He answered and listened.

"I've got relatives in Trinidad. We can go there, me, my baby and Jessi."

"What in the hell kind of dumb idea is that? You don't have passports," Charmaine blurted out. Then she sighed. "I'm sorry, it's just... I'm losing my grip right now."

"It's okay, Char," Diamond said. Then she grinned at Charmaine. "But we do have passports. Me and Jessi got 'em last year. We've been talking about a trip to my homeland for almost two years."

"Sweetie, I doubt that's a workable plan now," Charmaine said as she tucked a braid behind Diamond's ear.

Scotty walked over and broke into their conversation. "Right. You probably won't get out of this neighborhood, much less past airport security. The police are looking for all of us."

"Shit," Diamond hissed and tightly wrapped both arms around her curvy body.

Charmaine pulled out her cell phone. "I got a text from Keisha."

"What's she sayin'?" Scotty frowned.

"Gloating," Charmaine replied through clenched teeth and read the message aloud. "Little sis going 2 jail for murder. Got u bitch lol." Then the phone rang, this time playing Charmaine's favorite Jill Scott tune. She hit the green button and put it on speaker. Keisha's raucous laughter scraped Charmaine's eardrum.

"Every one of you is going to prison. Bye-bye-eee," Keisha sang and hung up.

"Uh-uh, we can't let her play us like this," Diamond burst out. She jumped up and down like a kid having a tantrum while her hands flapped wildly. "Let's call my brother Jon-Jon and 'nem. His boys will take her out."

"No," Charmaine said forcefully. She grabbed Diamond by the shoulders forcing her to be still. "We can't run around doing stupid stuff because we're in a panic. That's the best way to make things worse."

"Besides, the cops are already looking for Jessi; they've got her name and description. By now they know her family and friends, and their friends and relatives."

Scotty strode to the window, peeked out and came back to stand next to Charmaine.

"I gotta think," Charmaine said.

She resumed pacing for another ten minutes. Diamond slumped onto the floral sofa and stared ahead at nothing in particular. Scotty kept working his cell phone as he prowled through the house. He checked the backyard through the kitchen window and looked at the houses in the neighborhood. Finally, Charmaine stopped pacing. She glanced at her phone again, cursed and threw it on the sofa. Then she covered her face with both hands. Seconds later Charmaine's head jerked up and her hands dropped. She found Scotty in the kitchen sucking down a beer and nodding as he listened to a voice on his Bluetooth headset.

"Hold on a minute, Raheem," he said when Charmaine walked up to him fast.

"Have the cops gone to that hotel yet?" Charmaine asked.

"Hell yeah. We barely made it out before they did. My boys say they pulled up about ten minutes after we left."

Scotty hit his cell phone's mute button. "What are you thinking?"

"Can you find out what time the 911 call got to the cops, and what time they got there?" Charmaine reached out and clutched his arm. Her heart beat so hard her chest seemed to vibrate.

"Yeah, but what's that gonna do?" Scotty blinked at her rapidly.

"Just find out. I'm going to talk to Jessi. Be right back." Charmaine spun around and raced to the bedroom.

"Okay, but..." Scotty called out.

Charmaine kept going. Forty minutes later Charmaine and Jessi came back to the living room. Scotty walked in from the kitchen with a grimace on his dark, handsome face. Diamond stood up.

Charmaine wrapped an arm around Jessi. "We're going to give ourselves up to the police."

6.

Three hours later, just after midnight, Charmaine sat on a hard chair in the Seventh District Police Station on Dwyer Road. Jessi had been taken to a separate room. Obviously, the police didn't want them getting their stories lined up as they were questioned. Charmaine knew they'd sized up Jessi as the weakest link. Charmaine was worried about Jessi, but not for the reasons the police probably thought. This was a risky move, but they didn't have a better alternative. Jessi seemed beaten down and numb, as if all the years of misery had suddenly overwhelmed her.

Detective Harrison wore a powder blue NOPD shirt tucked into his black slacks. He gazed at her from his position in the chair opposite Charmaine. His expression seemed sympathetic. "Look, your sister is a little bitty girl. She must have felt threatened."

"She always feels threatened, detective. You get that way from being beaten and raped repeatedly before you make your sweet sixteen birthday." Charmaine glanced to her left at the wide mirrored glass set into the wall like a window. "Keisha Front on the other side, huh?"

"I know you and your sister had it real rough. Maybe this is a way you can get her some help," Detective Harrison replied, ignoring her question.

His words pricked at Charmaine. She let out a shaky sigh, but managed to hold onto her emotions and not cry. She wanted more than anything for Jessi to stop hurting, to live without drugging herself into oblivion. Charmaine stiffened her spine and steadied her breathing. She gazed back at him.

"You're hard-core. I get it," Detective Harrison said. He started to speak again, but stopped when the interview room door swung open. A tall white officer came in.

"The story checks out. Every detail," the police officer said and glanced at Charmaine.

Twenty minutes later Charmaine walked out between the two men. They went to a large room filled with desks. Police officers came and went looking serious. A few talked on the phone. When Jessi appeared accompanied by a policewoman, Charmaine rushed over and hugged her.

Charmaine brushed down her sister's tussled hair. "It's going to be okay. I promise."

Two other detectives ushered in Keisha and Lorenzo. Keisha glared at them. "This is a bunch of bullshit! What do you mean I need to 'go with this detective to an interview room'? I'm not going anywhere."

"They want to get our statements is all. Calm down," Lorenzo said firmly as his gaze darted back and forth. "Starting a riot up in here is not a good idea."

"They killed my poor husband. You need to arrest those two," Keisha yelled and brushed Lorenzo's hand from her arm. She pointed at Charmaine and then pressed a wad of tissues to her eyes, even though not one tear had fallen. "James wasn't a saint, but he didn't deserve to die because he picked up a psycho prostitute."

"Maybe they will arrest us for something, but not murder. Thanks for the text and phone call, Keisha," Charmaine spat out.

"What?" Keisha frowned, an expression of confusion twisting her face.

"I told you to shut the hell up," Lorenzo mumbled.

"I'm glad she's so talkative. The police wanna find out how you knew Jessi would be wanted for murder three minutes after the 911 operator got the call." Charmaine nodded as Keisha's mouth dropped open. "Yeah, and before the first cop found the body."

"She's lying!" Keisha shouted as two police officers led her away. "You gonna listen to her? Don't touch me! I've got friends, important people. I'm calling my lawyer."

"Look man," Lorenzo stammered and wiped a large hand over his face. "I don't know nothin' about nothin'. Okay? I'm just a friend who agreed to drive her down here so she could get justice. All I'm doing is tryin' to help the lady out. I haven't even known her that long," Lorenzo protested frantically. His voice faded as he was led away.

Jessi leaned her head on Charmaine's shoulder. "I'm so tired, Char."

"We'll be home soon, sweetie," Charmaine said quietly and kissed the top of her tangled curls.

"How did you know the Front's house had cameras installed inside?" Detective Harrison asked Charmaine. His dark eyebrows went up giving him a suspicious expression.

"They live in a lovely home, nice area but we have a high crime rate. Makes sense don't you think?" Charmaine kept her expression neutral.

"That thing about Mrs. Front texting you was shaky, circumstantial, even if it was suspicious. The video of her and Thomas hauling what looks like a body out of the house is going to be harder for them to explain. You two dodged a bullet this go round. I strongly suggest you help your sister change her lifestyle, ma'am." Detective Harrison said, bass voice pitched deep with intensity as he made his point.

"Yes, sir," Charmaine said and pulled Jessi against her protectively.

7.

The next morning Scotty and Diamond sat in Charmaine's kitchen at the table in an alcove. The cheerful yellow and green decor contrasted greatly with the dark hours they'd spent earlier. Sunshine streamed through the windows above the sink. Scotty shoved a mound of eggs into his mouth. Diamond munched on a slice of bacon. Diamond's little girl sat in a chair with a fist full of grits. She was happily getting more food on her face than in her mouth.

"I'm glad to see the sun come up on a new day," Charmaine said. "That's a blues song my last foster mother used to sing. And that's exactly how I feel."

"Jessi is still knocked out. I mean she looks like she's in a coma," Diamond said as she tried to wipe her toddler's cheeks clean.

"Once she finally felt safe, Jessi could relax," Charmaine replied calmly.

"She's right, Diamond. I've seen big strong dudes do the same thing. They just fall out after running on adrenalin for hours, even days," Scotty added.

"Don't worry, Diamond. We're all going to be okay." Charmaine wiped her hands on the kitchen towel. Then she blew a kiss at little Indyah.

Scotty wiped his mouth with a paper napkin and sat back. "By the way, Charmaine, how did you know that Front had hidden video cameras in his house?"

"Humph, he knew Keisha was up to no good I bet," Diamond put in and continued swabbing down her squirming toddler.

Charmaine leaned against the counter. "I didn't. Jessi told me."

Scotty wore a baffled expression as he digested her reply for a few seconds. "Wait a minute, Jessi knew Front before?"

"No," Charmaine said.

"Then how..." Scotty blinked exchanged a glance with Diamond who shrugged.

"James Leland Front told Jessi. The dead seem drawn to her, those who can't move on and want to tell their stories. I had to hypnotize her to get the details."

"Damn," Scotty and Diamond exclaimed in unison.

"Keisha and Lorenzo will go to prison for a long time. Too bad about Lorenzo, cause he was good company. At least I got that little bonus before I had to burn him," Charmaine said. She grinned at them and went back to washing the breakfast dishes.

Hunting Spirits

1.
The Grand Intro

Charmaine moved slowly through the nineteenth century mansion. Noise from traffic on St. Charles Avenue in New Orleans only a block away contrasted with the otherworldly atmosphere inside. The muffled swish of cars and rumble of delivery trucks sounded odd. Late afternoon sunshine slanted through windows, the heavy drapes pulled back. Still, deep brown antique furniture made the house seem dark.

"This is beyond creepy. Don't know how I let you talk me into this," Jessi mumbled.

She glanced at a window to her left. "Real cozy, if you're like haunted houses where people end up dead."

"Anything?" Charmaine said, ignoring her sister's complaints.

"Dead men tell no tales," Jessi replied. Then she went into a fit of giggles. "Get it? That old saying..."

"Yeah, I get it. Will you focus please? We're here to do a job. Mrs. Fortsall paid a hefty fee for us to get rid of her problem. And no smoking," Charmaine added when she saw Jessi fishing in the pocket of her leather Moto jacket.

"I'm cutting back. Nicotine gum." Jessi held up a small square then popped it into her mouth. She chewed for a few seconds.

"Humph." Charmaine cracked a brief smile. She went back to scanning the large parlor for signs of paranormal activity.

She dared not bring too much attention to her younger sister's new healthy routine. Jessi breathed rebellion. Any sign that Charmaine was turning into an authority figure could trigger an outbreak. Still Charmaine relished having Jessi as a sidekick. Away from her dangerous lifestyle of drugs and prostitution, Jessi became a funny intelligent twenty-something taking online college courses. Her sister deserved a good life after the childhood she'd been through; the hell they'd both been through as kids. Maybe they could end up with normal lives after all. When they weren't taking gigs to track down troublesome things that go bump in the night. Or day. Charmaine paused. Then she swung around as if to extend her invisible psychic antennae.

"Did you hear a noise?"

"Probably a cat in the alley. Hate those things. Relax," Jessi drawled. "Going upstairs."

"Sounded like something dragging across the floor upstairs, not a cat. Be careful. Maybe Mrs. Fontaine is just a superstitious lady with a bit of paranoia tossed in. But you never know." Charmaine walked to a glass cabinet. Crystal and blown glass figurines stared back at her. A collection of animals and tiny people seemed to question what she was doing disturbing them. "Fortune worth of doo-dads just on one shelf."

"Huh?" Jessi's said over a shoulder just as she went through an archway to the hall.

"Nothing." Charmaine figured it best not to give little sis ideas for bringing in extra income. She wasn't totally reformed yet.

"Yes, mother," Jessi wisecracked. "Damn. This staircase is bigger than the shotgun house we grew up in."

"The closets are bigger than the house we grew up in," Charmaine joked to herself, because she was alone downstairs.

Totally alone. Nothing moved except leaves on the house plant stirred by the cool air from heating vents. The formal living room looked like something out of Architectural Digest. Rich dark oak tables and chairs contrasted with oak wood floors in a lighter color. Not that much of the floors could be seen. Beautiful cream and ruby red wool rugs covered them. Pale green draperies were pulled back from the windows. Cream gauzy curtains beneath the draperies let in light but kept a private feel. Charmaine gave up resisting the urge to touch the rich fabrics of the sofas. A few leather chairs were mixed in as well.

She moved across the hallway that bisected the mansion. A long formal dining room that doubled as a ballroom took her breath away. She marveled that people actually lived like this. She glanced up at the elaborate crystal and gold chandelier. The plaster of Paris ceiling was painted in a pattern that complimented the enormous wool rug. A table capable of seating twenty-five people stretched down the center. More chairs lined the walls. Beautiful and untouched. That's what felt weird. The place didn't feel lived in. She moved through the other rooms and picked up human vibes, especially in the kitchen.

"Probably the cook or hired caterers for her parties," Charmaine said aloud to no one. Still it was spotless with everything in place.

The sprawling library was a different matter. Raw male energy filled the room.

Two walls contained large bookcases. A narrow yet sturdy looking staircase on one wall led up to a balcony with another bookcase. Furniture just as rich filled the room. The massive oak desk dominated the room. Along another wall a set in credenza held a computer with two monitors and another chair. An oil portrait of a stern looking man hung over the fireplace.

"My husband's domain," a husky female voice said firmly.

Charmaine started and spun around. "Shit, I almost..."

"What?" The tall auburn-haired woman strolled in with one professionally perfect eyebrow raised.

No need to say she almost pulled a gun and shot her crazy ass, which was on the tip of Charmaine's tongue. Rule number five on Charmaine's small business tip list – don't shoot your client; especially one with deep pockets. Your creditors will not be pleased.

"Sorry Mrs. Forstall. I thought you'd be gone until at least seven tonight,"

Charmaine said, recovering quickly. Images of bills due helped her overcome being royally pissed by the woman. Again.

Mrs. Forstall chuckled deep in her throat. She shrugged and tossed her purse onto a nearby chair. Then she crossed to the bar. "I got curious about how ghost hunters work. Can you get rid of whatever is menacing this house today?"

"We're not 'ghost hunters'. And I'm afraid it doesn't work like that," Charmaine drawled. The woman must have majored in annoying the lower classes at her fancy private school.

"Well how does it work then?" Mrs. Forstall gracefully turned to Charmaine again. She held a tumbler of brandy in one hand.

"We assess security first off. You'd be surprised at how many 'ghostly' happenings turn out to be a crime about to take place." Charmaine continued to circle the room, examining objects at she went.

"Something is stalking me in my own home," Mrs. Forstall said.

Charmaine looked at her sharply. Loretta Chevalier Forstall wasn't joking, nor was she play-acting. Her hand shook as she raised the glass to her mouth. Born into one of the old New Orleans families, she'd married into another equally distinguished old family. Mrs. Forstall was still on the sunny side of forty; at thirty-seven she was only eight years older than Charmaine.

"So far we haven't found anything, not one sinister whisper. No objects floating on their own. No heavy footsteps," Charmaine said. She turned back to gaze at the leather bound books.

"Don't patronize me, Ms. Joliet," Mrs. Forstall snapped. "I'm not some elderly nincompoop with too much time on my hands and a wild imagination."

Charmaine took a deep breath and faced Mrs. Forstall. "I'm sorry. I didn't mean to sound like I was making fun of you. I can see your fear is real. Let's go over what's been happening again.

Mrs. Forstall blinked back tears. She put a hand to her forehead and then sat down on a leather sofa nearby. "Do I have to?"

"Being here might help you think of details you didn't recall at my office." Charmaine sat beside her and assumed a sympathetic expression. "No rush, just take it slow."

"For the past three months I haven't felt comfortable here. Not since my husband... went to oversee the Rome branch of his business."

Charmaine and Jessi figured that was code for he left her for another woman. But they were still checking out the family and her story. "He took your children with him."

"No, Alyssa only. Grayson is away at school. I told you all of this." Mrs. Forstall glanced at Charmaine. "You're checking to see if I keep my story straight."

"You've been shaken up. I want to make sure I have it right. That's all." Charmaine said with a business-like nod. "Go on."

"Grayson was accepted into Williams College. I thought he was too young to go so far from home, but my husband disagreed." Mrs. Forstall's expression turned sour. She finished off the drink and frowned at the empty glass.

"You didn't mind your youngest going to Italy?" Charmaine tilted her head to one side as if the angle would afford clear insight.

"She'd never been abroad, and she adores her father," Mrs. Forstall said in a flat tone. "You said 'we'. I hired you. I don't want strangers mixing in my personal affairs."

"My sister—"

"Isn't part of our business arrangement," Mrs. Forstall said crisply and stood, drink in hand. She started to say more, but a loud thump stopped her. She dropped the glass. "Oh God. It's starting before daylight now, that horrible sound."

"I doubt it," Charmaine murmured. She stood and walked to the open door leading to hallway.

"I hear it. We have to get out. Now!" Mrs. Forstall's already pale coloring turned almost glowing white.

"Don't scream. We're not going to let anything bad happen to you." Charmaine crossed to the woman and shoved her down onto the sofa again. "Stay put."

Mrs. Forstall's mouth worked but no words came out. Fear had disconnected her brain to her vocal chords it seemed. Charmaine felt a rush of energy as well, but not fear. She'd given up being scared of the supernatural. People and the things they got up to sent more chills down her spine than any goblin. She'd been on the receiving end enough times.

With a hand in the leather cross-body bag slung over one shoulder, Charmaine stepped into the hallway. The wide staircase looked stunning as usual. A louder banging sound came from upstairs. As Charmaine put a foot on the first carpeted stair, Jessi appeared on the landing above, hands on both hips.

"The rich bitch lied to you. There's a body up here, and it sure is hell ain't natural causes."

2. The Plot Gets Thick

Two hours later Detective Wayne Harrison stood with a cigar clamped between his lips. The color of milk chocolate and at least six feet tall, Detective Harrison's gaze missed little. He huffed and puffed smoke as he observed the chaos spread out before him. Night had fallen, and the cold March evening wind made him pulled his wool jacket closer. Police lights flashed casting blue against the stately old home. Harrison took turns glaring at Charmaine and listening to verbal reports from other officers. What Charmaine assumed were two crime scene techs went in and out of the house. After thirty minutes they returned with plastic and paper bags. The body had not been moved. After another thirty minutes Harrison marched over to Charmaine.

"Where's my sister? She's sensitive around cops you know," Charmaine said, pre-empting his control of what would become a police interview.

"Yeah, that happens when you run around killing folks," Harrison growled back.

"She's never been convicted or even arrested." Charmaine leaned against the NOPD cruiser and crossed her ankles.

"Dead bodies and you two young ladies seem to attract each other. Now we've got another one." Harrison jerked a thumb toward the Forstall mansion.

"Sadly violent crime is a problem in our wonderful city, Detective. Not that I blame the police. You folks are doing your best," Charmaine replied mildly.

"I... You little...." Harrison pointed a forefinger at Charmaine, but cut off his tirade. He glanced to his left and snorted. A pudgy white man in a dark suit beckoned to the detective. His attitude clearly showed he expected to be obeyed.

"Detective, we need to talk."

"Your boss gotta a lot of nerve," Charmaine prodded.

"Just stay right here. Keep your mouth shut about spirits and that other bullshit." Harrison strode off.

Harrison and the man entered into a tense exchange. Charmaine could tell they didn't like each other. Though interested in that dynamic, Charmaine worried more about Jessi. Her sister had a flat out phobia about police officers. Ignoring the detective's order, Charmaine went to two police cars, but Jessi wasn't in either of them. Then she spotted her. The double doors of a police van were open. Jessi sat in the van with a blanket around her. She held a plastic cup. As Charmaine cautiously approached, Jessi winked.

"What the...?" Charmaine whispered once she got close.

"I felt faint from the shock of finding a dead woman, so the nice officer helped me. Then he got my preliminary statement." Jessi sipped from the cup. "Want some water? I got connections."

"Harrison is here and he's pissed. Thinks we're up to our necks in this murder." Charmaine sighed as she sat next Jessi.

"Yeah, that's Commander Murphy with him. Mrs. Got Mad Money is probably tossing us under the bus right this minute." Jessi turned to stare into the van. "Hmm, interesting tools."

"Keep your sticky fingers off. We're in enough deep shit as it is. And there's no way Mrs. Forstall can blame us for a dead body in her house." Charmaine bit her lip.

"Power and privilege. She hired us to sniff out the hired help stealing. We confronted her housekeeper, there was a fight and now there's a dead body. We have shady records." Jessi shrugged.

"You have a history of attacking people, not me. I just have a history of..." Charmaine's voice trailed off.

"You have a history of getting me out of trouble. Who you think they gonna believe?" Jessi gave a grunt.

"Wait, the victim is a woman and her employee? How did you find out?" Charmaine craned her neck until she spotted Detective Harrison. He and Commander Murphy still faced off.

"She didn't tell me," Jessi said. She shrugged again when Charmaine glanced at her sharply. "Hey, not all ghosts hang around to chat. Some spirits take off to wherever they go once the body stops."

"Heaven or hell," Charmaine said.

"There you go with the religion myths. One day we'll have a scientific explanation for a lot of paranormal activity. Our bodies generate energy. Ghosts or spirits are probably some form of subatomic particles generated after we die." Jessi waved a hand. "Stop with the God and angels crap."

"Who created those particles? Okay, look. Let's debate intelligent design later.

So some cute police officer gave you information?" Charmaine looked at Jessi.

"I acted like I knew more than I did, which wasn't hard. The woman has on a uniform, like a hotel housekeeper. Dark blue pants and a matching button front shirt." Jessi drained the rest of the water from the cup and tossed it into the van.

"Please tell me you didn't touch a dead body," Charmaine blurted out.

"I checked to see if the poor heffa was still breathing. Not that it was likely since Shawntelle was stuffed in the wall." Jessi patted her jacket pocket. She sighed happily as she pulled out a package of cigarettes.

Charmaine snatched them from her. "How did you know her... oh."

"Right. This house was built between 1849 and 1852. Any place that old has to have a little something extra floating around. A slave named Lucas wanders the neighborhood. He worked for one her hubby's ancestors. Did carpentry work when his owner let him. Says both families are a mean bunch," Jessi said.

"I'll listen to hundred year old gossip another time. So he knows how she ended up dead?" Charmaine gazed at the house. The beauty of it started to fade with each secret uncovered.

"He wasn't around. Lucas was down the street scaring the shit out of a descendant of a man who used to beat slaves for fun," Jessi said with a wide grin.

"No wonder you two got along. So how did she die?" Charmaine stood and stretched. The last few hours had started to take a toll. Her legs ached.

"Read some minds and find out for shit's sake. I can't do all the work," Jessi retorted.

"Very funny," Charmaine snapped.

"I hacked through the wall with a heavy silver vase. The plaster or whatever seemed mighty thin, like an old closet covered over. I think she was shot." Jessi started to say more, but broke off and nodded. "Here we go."

Charmaine turned around to see Harrison and his boss coming their way."Let me do the talking."

"Gladly," Jessi retorted. She pulled the blanket around her as if for protection.

"Didn't I say stay put?" Harrison drew his shoulders in at the look his boss gave him.

"The situation should be under your control, Harrison," the man cracked. He gave Charmaine and Jessi an appraising glace for a few seconds in silence. "You two are free to go. Handle it, Harrison."

"Yes sir," Harrison spat.

The man lingered only a second to eye the detective before he strode off. "I'll get with you later," he called without looking back.

Detective Harrison faced Charmaine and Jessi. "You have more luck than a bucket of four leaf clovers."

"Oh good, we're not murder suspects," Jessi quipped in a dry tone. She hopped down from the back of the van and tossed the police blanket on the floor board. "Let's get the hell outta here before they change their minds, Charmaine."

"Wait a minute." Charmaine frowned and blink rapidly.

"Your baby sister is right. Be glad you've been handed a get-out-of-jail-free," Harrison said.

"But..." Charmaine pointed at the house.

"Go away," Harrison barked loud and both women jumped. Then he lowered his voice. "You've got something on this uptown chick with big political connections. I'm going to find out what you're up to, Ms. Joliet. Until then, don't come unless I send for you."

"I'm not up to anything. She called us." Charmaine stopped when Harrison's eyes turned to slits.

"You're absolutely right, detective. We should get out of your way so you can do your job. Come on Charmaine." Jessi grabbed Charmaine's arm. After a few insistent tugs, she finally got them both moving.

"Something funny is going on." Charmaine matched Jessi's steps, but she kept looking back at Detective Harrison.

Jessi yanked her hard until they reached Charmaine's blue Ford Focus. "What was your first clue? A rich woman full of secrets and a spooky house, or the dead body in the wall?"

"Leaving might be a good idea for now," Charmaine muttered.

3. The Man with a Plan

One night later Charmaine looked into the barrel of the automatic pistol pointed at her. The round hole where a bullet might come out any second seemed huge. The man holding it blurred into a scary background figure in the dark. So maybe it wasn't a coincidence that the light under her carport had gone out.

He'd come up behind Charmaine before she could get inside the door leading to her kitchen. He ordered her to shut up and go inside fast. His deep voice had a dreamy lover boy quality. Except he wasn't trying to charm anyone, certainly not Charmaine. Who? Why? Wait, not a priority at the moment.

"And don't try sayin' you ain't by yourself," her unwelcome visitor rumbled. "Get away from the door. I said move!"

"Look, I have more bills than money. But I got eighty dollars stashed in that big cookie jar. Grocery money for my family. I'm just tryin' to make it like everybody else," Charmaine said, putting a tremble in her voice.

"Humph. You ain't got no kids, so don't try the single mother angle. We not goin' to the kitchen so you can get your hands on a knife or somethin'. Move down that hall. We're goin' to the living room. No, wait. We goin' in your office Miss social worker." The man waved the gun at her to walk.

Charmaine thought fast as they walked through the door and down the hallway. He had done his homework on her. "You can tell I don't have much worth stealing by looking around. I have two televisions, an old computer and not much else."

"Yeah. I oughta jack your raggedy shit as payment for the trouble you caused me. But I don't want your piddly-assed stuff. Put the purse down on this table and go over there."

"Okay, sure." Charmaine kept her back to him as she placed her purse down and walked across the room.

"Turn around," the man ordered.

"I haven't seen your face or even what you're wearing, so I can't describe you to..."

"Turn around," the said with more edge to his tone.

With a deep sigh, Charmaine faced him slowly. The fact that he didn't care if she saw his face was seriously bad news. He had no intention of leaving her alive to tell the tale. "You don't want to rob me, so now what?"

The man was the color of honey. His dark tight curls were cut close. He glanced around the room for a few seconds. Then he focused on Charmaine gain. He seemed quite comfortable holding a gun on another human being. "I'm Darrius James, the one you and that rich woman set up for

Shawntelle's murder. Yeah, I see the light bulb just went on over your head."

"We didn't, I mean I didn't set you up for murder. You have a history of getting into fights with Mrs. Forstall's housekeeper. You came to the house while Shawntelle was at work and threatened her. It's... it's in the police files. Once they identified her—"

"I only went to her job twice without calling, and Shawntelle threatened me for showing up," Darrius broke in.

"Uh, y'all got into a fist fight at a nightclub last year. The police report says you had a knife."

"I ain't stupid enough to kill her and leave the body at that bitch's house," Darrius growled. "If I took somebody out wouldn't be nothin' left for them CSI types to find."

"Okay, just explain to the cops," Charmaine said weakly. She flinched when Darrius let out a growly laugh empty of amusement.

"Sure. Big black guy with a record goes to the cops and explains they got it all wrong. He didn't kill his girlfriend. That oughta work real good." Darrius glanced at his watch. "I got a much better idea."

Charmaine glanced at the digital clock on her desk. The glowing red numbers told her it was almost ten o'clock. "Um, what would that be?"

"Shawntelle told me more than once her boss is crazy. All kinds of nasty secrets in that family," Darrius said.

"Like?"

"Did Miz Society Lady tell you we had us a three way one time?" Darrius grinned at Charmaine's gaping mouth. "Yeah, she swung both ways. Me, her and Shawntelle had us a party one weekend. Her husband and kids went to their beach house in Florida. Loretta pretended she was sick and stayed home. Bet when she was gabbing to the police she didn't tell 'em that story."

"I'm fairly sure she left it out," Charmaine murmured. "So Mrs. Forstall invited you inside at least once."

Darrius grinned and winked. "Musta been good to her cause I got invited back

two more times. I think she liked Shawntelle better than me."

"And you weren't..."

"Jealous? Hell no, I don't judge. Besides,
Shawntelle was just in it for the money.
Got a nice cash bonus and expensive liq-
uor to take home." Darrius grunted a sigh.
"I'm gonna miss that girl."

"How sentimental of you," Charmaine
muttered. She looked around her office.
For the first time she realized how few escape routes it had. Once she earned the
rest of her fee she'd do renovations. "Look,
I go wherever the facts lead. I'm not going
to help Mrs. Forstall cover up a crime, sure
as hell not murder. The police are suspicious about us anyway."

"What you mean 'us'?" Darrius squinted
at her.

"Um, me and Mrs. Forstall," Charmaine
said quickly. No point in putting a target
on Jessi.

"Yeah, well you can investigate the hell
out of her house tonight because we're going over there," Darrius said.

"Are you crazy? The cops still have that place roped off as a crime scene. You must want to be caught," Charmaine argued.

Darrius shook his head. "The cops finished up this morning. Mrs. Forstall is back in the house. The cleaning service she called been there all day."

"Right, of course." Charmaine shot him a sideways glance before she went back to plotting against him.

"You ain't gettin' away from me. We gone leave here in another half hour and surprise the bitch. I'll get her to talk." Darrius motioned at her with the gun. "So sit down."

"Sure thing, Darrius. Your plan makes all kinds of sense. The moment she sees you, Loretta is going to confess and let me record everything on my cell phone. We'll be home by midnight." Charmaine slumped down into another chair across from him.

"Ya think?" Darrius quipped. Then he managed to pull out a cigarette, put it in his mouth and light it with the gun still pointed at her chest.

Forty-five minutes later Charmaine started to get antsy. Darrius was on his fourth cigarette when his cell phone played a tune. He dropped the cigarette and crushed it into her laminate floors. For that alone Charmaine decided to get revenge.

"Humph. We're clear to head over there. You're driving, and you know I can use this gun like a pro. Right?" Darrius stood.

"I guessed as much, yeah," Charmaine replied.

She didn't have any silly notions about running since those bullets would be faster. So Charmaine decided to take a chance on following orders. At least he had a destination in mind. Darrius could still decide to make her drive to her own burial site, but Charmaine didn't think so.

After twenty minutes of driving carefully and obeying all traffic laws, they arrived at the Garden District mansion. Charmaine looked around for increased private security in vain. Maybe a patrol car would be circling, but no.

"They think I'm in New Orleans east. Paid somebody to call in a tip. So the don't' expect the cops," Darrius said quietly. He lay down on the back seat just in case, the gun still on Charmaine.

"She's probably staying with a friend or a relative. Mrs. Forstall was already scared to be in the house alone because—"

"There's some kind of ghost or something in the house. Why doesn't she sell the place? Because she's full of bullshit, that's why." Darrius sat straight. "Don't park in the circular driveway. Pull down the one that leads to the back."

Charmaine drove down the side of the house. She stopped at the end of the driveway. A lovely two story carriage house sat adjacent to the main house. A Porsche SUV sat in the three car garage. A tall lamppost threw yellow light across the rear lawn. Darrius left the backseat first, then waved her out.

"I'm telling you this is a bad idea. Mrs. Forstall is scared out of her mind. She might shoot us on sight," Charmaine said.

Darrius handed Charmaine a throw away cell phone. "She's here by herself. That alone tells you she ain't scared. Loretta is a planner. She killed Shawntelle for a reason, and I wanna know why. I'll get us through the back door. Tell her you're at the front door. You didn't want to alarm her, that's why you called. Say you found some important evidence."

Charmaine made a sudden move at a shuffling sound to her right. "What was that?"

"You better not be jumping around while I'm holding this gun. Now call." Darrius grabbed Charmaine from behind and pressed it into her side. Then he took the cell from her. "I put a silencer on. Point blank will muffle the shot even more."

"You... you planning to kill us?" Charmaine shivered.

"I'm still working that part out. Now walk."

Darrius used a key to get into the house and ease them into the kitchen. He disarmed the alarm. Charmaine fumbled with the phone and tapped the number. Mrs. Forstall answered on the fourth ring. Though surprised, she seemed relieved to hear from Charmaine.

"Silly bitch didn't even think to change the code. Now let's go surprise her."

Mrs. Forstall was still at the front door in the wide foyer when they approached from behind. She stifled a short yelp and whirled to face them. Then she let out a slow breath. "Miss Joliet, it's you thank God. I thought... oh never mind. But how did you get inside? I don't understand."

Darrius stepped from the shadows still holding the gun, a second man with him. "Nice to see you again, Loretta. Let's go the library."

4. He Had It Comin'

The heavy drapes in the library closed, Darrius went about serving himself and his friend Zed a drink. Zed held a revolver on them as he glanced around. He seemed more interested in sizing up items he could steal. Charmaine tried to calm her nerves enough so she could think straight. Hard to do with two pissed off gangstas holding pistols and winging it with what they would do with their hostages. Finally, she decided to ask.

"I don't get the point of all this, Darrius. Mrs. Forstall—"

"Call her Loretta. No need to be all formal now that we're hangin' out," Darrius cut in.

"You're just piling up felonies by kidnapping and assaulting us. You know the police are looking everywhere for you. They'll see through the fake tip real quick," Charmaine continued.

"You give them too much credit," Zed replied. He glanced over to make sure Darrius had his gun up again. Then he set about examining a tall glazed vase.

"Loretta is gonna tell us what happened to Shawntelle. I mean the damn truth," Darrius barked before Mrs. Forstall could reply.

"She must have stayed late to finish up. I'd asked her to polish the copper bowls and plates that belonged to my mother. I didn't even realize she was still in the house. Poor thing. I warned her."

"I warned her not to trust you," Darrius snapped.

Mrs. Forstall gazed at Zed for a few seconds then looked at Darrius. "The police called with more information. Shawntelle wasn't killed with a gun. Your sister was wrong, Ms. Joliet."

"Sister?" Darrius glanced sharply at Charmaine.

"We work together once in a while. She doesn't know anything," Charmaine said.

"I'll find out what she knows later. Now you tell us what the police said." Darrius settled into a large leather chair.

"The blood came from strange wounds on her body. His throat was crushed and... it's too horrible." Mrs. Forstall placed at hand on her own neck and shuddered visibly. "It's getting worse."

Zed looked up from the Chinese porcelain bowl he held. "What's gettin' worse? What's she talking about, D?"

"Some kind of ghost or supernatural entity in the house," Charmaine put in before Mrs. Forstall answered. "Something strong."

"Bull.Shit." Darrius gulped down the rest of the expensive bourbon. "Ignore that playacting, Zed."

"I heard stories about these old houses." Zed dropped the bowl with a thud on the cherry wood table.

Charmaine winced as the vase next to it wobbled and then steadied. She exhaled. "Don't break up your profit. The stuff won't be worth anything in pieces."

Mrs. Forstall took a step then stopped when Darrius pointed the gun at her. "You can take whatever you want. Those two pieces alone are worth over fifteen thousand dollars."

"Hell no. Like we're stupid enough to get caught trying to unload 'em."

"I won't report them stolen. I can give you the name of a dealer who'll pay top dollar. I'll say you're acting as my agents." Mrs. Forstall nodded to Zed.

"Hey, sounds like a sweet deal." Zed looked at Darius. "We have her write a note to the dealer. What about antique jewelry?"

"I only have three pieces here. The rest are in our bank deposit box. But the necklace, earrings and ring are eighteen karat gold. They're Cartier made in 1925, yellow diamonds," Mrs. Forstall said quickly.

"Nice," Zed said, his nervousness about talk of ghosts and goblins forgotten.

"We ain't after no petty cash," Darrius snapped. "Shawntelle said there's a safe upstairs concealed in a closet. Rich folks had ways of hiding their goods from the help back then. She says there is money and jewels in there. And more."

"She was wrong," Mrs. Forstall blurted out and twisted her hands. "My husband moved everything to the bank."

"Somehow I don't believe you, Loretta. Shawntelle came back while you were out. She was about to make off with the goods and expose your dirty skeletons, so you killed her," Darrius snarled.

"Damn," Charmaine muttered and turned to Mrs. Forstall.

Mrs. Forstall dropped her hands at her sides. "That's ridiculous. No one, especially the police, will buy your story."

"Must be some good stuff up there." Zed looked at the ceiling with a hungry expression.

"And she won't report it missing either. Will you Loretta?" Darrius gave a laugh. "You'll go down for murder, and the cops will think you fenced your own junk."

"You have no idea how stupid you sound," Mrs. Forstall snapped. She lifted her chin. "No one will believe a ghetto rat instead of me."

Darrius chuckled deep in his throat. "Zed, go upstairs, turn right and find a set of stairs to a third floor. There's another big bedroom at the end of a hallway. To the left. Open the double doors on the big upright dresser. Look on the right for circle. Press it and a panel will slid back."

"Got it." Zed strode out on a mission. The soft thump of his footsteps on the stairs, and then on the second floor landing followed seconds later.

Mrs. Forstall glanced at the doorway Zed had gone through. "Don't be a fool. I can make you richer than a few thousand dollars and a few trinkets."

"Charmaine, wanna hear more secrets?" Darrius continued to gaze at Mrs. Forstall. "Her precious son has a little, make that a big drug habit. I should know. He was my best customer. Mr. Forstall works a lot, plus he's not the family man type. Anyway Loretta managed to hide the embarrassing truth from him. Not hard since Mr. F. and the kid can't stand each other. Her husband is glad not to see the kid."

"Shut up. You don't know anything about my family," Mrs. Forstall hissed at him, a look of upper-class scorn twisting her mouth down.

"Anyway, Mr. Forstall, Hamilton, his buddies call him Ham. So good old Ham is just as happy to be away from home and ignorant of what all goes down around here. Except he loves his baby girl, the kid; not the wife." Darrius got up and refilled his drink. He still held the gun expertly to show he could plug both of them for moving the wrong way.

"What's that?" Mrs. Forstall said, her voice shaky as she looked at the open door.

"I didn't hear anything," Charmaine replied. Still she glanced around the room checking for strange movement.

"Hey, don't interrupt. I'm getting to the good parts. See, the first born is probably not Ham's kid. But Ham, he don't know this or even suspect." Darrius gave a grunt. "Loretta, you really need to ease up on the drinks when you party with us ghetto rats. I wasn't so high I didn't remember the juicy details."

"Hey, I found it. Damn, you was right. But it's too much to move by myself," Zed called from upstairs.

Darrius rolled his eyes and walked to the library door. "Don't be a dumbass. I can't leave these two alone."

"Tie 'em up then. This shit is heavy," Zed complained with a loud grunt.

"Make extra trips, man. We can't take no chances." Darrius looked at the women and lowered his voice. "See what I gotta deal with?"

Charmaine snorted. "Yeah, I'm feeling so sorry for you."

"Hey, D. I'm tellin' you, there's more up here than you thought. Hell, just go ahead and shoot up now so we can get outta here fast." Zed's voice faded as he moved away.

A loud thump and a dragging sound followed.

"Quit whinin' like a lil' bitch and get the stuff," Darrius yelled back. He turned his attention back to the ladies. "Even with you killin' my girl, I still kinda like you Loretta."

"I didn't kill Shawntelle you idiot. Listen to me before we're all dead," Mrs. Forstall snapped.

"And Miss Charmaine, you fine as hell. But thing is y'all what they call a liability right about now." Darrius shrugged an apology.

"We'll be a death penalty liability if you make your situation worse by killing us. You've got reasonable doubt on your side with Shawntelle's murder. The police can't place you near the house the day we found her. Get some of your friends to alibi you," Charmaine spoke quickly.

"Hmm, good points. Except we need time to get away with our property," Darrius said.

Charmaine started to finish her argument to save their lives when a strangled squealed cut through the air. A gurgling noise filled the house. More thumps. The squealing rose to a pitched keening. Darrius looked at the two women as he moved to hallway.

"Zed, quit messing around and get your ass down here. Zed!" Darrius licked his lips. The only response was the thudding of an object down the wide staircase.

"You have a gun. Go help your friend before it's too late." Mrs. Forstall's voice shook.

"What are you talking about?" Charmaine felt a cold chill spread from her neck down her arms. "Uh, Darrius, let's follow Mrs. Forstall's advice and leave. Now."

Darrius waved the gun at them. "You two move over here where I can see you. Close together. Try anything and I'll shoot you both."

They did as he demanded, though Charmaine didn't want to stand close to Mrs. Forstall. Not because of the gun. Something strange and malevolent emanated from the woman. Or maybe she attracted evil. Dread crawled up Charmaine's spine making it hard for her to concentrate enough to read Mrs. Forstall. Nothing. She couldn't "see" the woman's thoughts. Fear blocked Charmaine's psychic ability. Mrs. Forstall gripped hers arm with a hand like biting cold ice.

"We have to get out of here or we'll end up like Zed," she whispered into Charmaine's ear.

"End up like..."

"Zed, quit actin' a fool and let's go."

Darrius eyed them and aimed at Mrs. Forstall's head. He scowled a warning without speaking. Then he darted a quick glance up the staircase. Then he disappeared into the shadows. He came back holding something. His eyes went wide when he came into the light.

"What the fuck... what the fuck."

Darrius howled and threw the object into the library, frantic to get it away from him. Mrs. Forstall gasped. She backed up fast dragging Charmaine with her. A bloody athletic shoe bounced and rolled across the carpet; a foot attached to the ankle still in it.

5. And Then There Was One

"Let me get this straight. Two burglars broke in Mrs. Forstall's house, and a ghost killed one 'em. Nothing left but a few body parts," Detective Harrison drawled and shook his head.

"Just a leg, like half a leg," Charmaine said. She huffed in frustration. "We're wasting time. Let's go get a killer."

Harrison, dressed in pullover sweater and slacks, gave the uniformed officer in the interview room with them a side-eye. The man hunched his shoulders and said nothing. Harrison glanced at his watch.

"Okay, this happened around midnight. So what have you been doing? That was...almost two hours ago. I know because they got me out of bed to come here, for this."

"I calmed Mrs. Forstall down and took her to stay with a friend over by City Park. She didn't want to disturb any of her neighbors." Charmaine bit her lip. "Yes, it sounds crazy, but you know how she is."

"Uh-huh, and I'm learning about you, too. Ms. Joliet," Detective Harrison said as he stifled a yawn.

"Send somebody to her house, man. It's a crime scene." Charmaine waved her arms.

"We know how to do our jobs. Get back to your story, and start from part where you helped a known criminal break into her house." Detective Harrison crossed his arms.

"I was kidnapped at gunpoint," Charmaine hissed at him. "Darrius, Shawntelle's boyfriend, wanted to make Mrs. Forstall admit she killed Shawntelle, and he wanted to steal from her. Zed, his pal, met up with him there."

"Zed, right." Detective Harrison looked at the notepad in front of him. "Got it."

"We heard a freaky noise upstairs, Zed was gurgling or choking. I don't know. His leg came down the stairs and..." Charmaine shuddered at the image that popped into her head.

"Just take your time. I know we've been over this already, but you talked a mile a minute. We want to make sure we got your account straight." Harrison glanced at the uniformed cop again.

"Sure. Darrius must have hit the front door at a dead run. He was screaming his head off, I know that. Mrs. Forstall pulled me through some French doors in the library. Darrius didn't think to take my keys from me. So me and Mrs. Forstall ran down the driveway. But instead of getting in my car she kept running. I can't blame after what we saw. I caught up with her and managed to get her into my car. There's a small private street behind the house. Thank God I didn't have to back out past that haunted mansion." Charmaine blew out a breath and fell back in her chair.

Harrison started to speak, but a knock on the door interrupted him. He got up, mumbled to someone, then he and the officer left. Charmaine resisted looking at the wide dark glass set into the wall to her left. No doubt cops stood on the other side of the two way mirror. They were probably taking bets on whether drugs or insanity contributed to her story. She didn't care. They'd find out soon enough.

Harrison came back with another plain-clothes detective. "My partner Detective Young. Okay, keep going. You came here to report the crime."

"Well, uh, I went back to the neighborhood to see if I would find Darrius. I mean cause he was on foot, right?" Charmaine cleared her throat.

"Oh that makes plenty sense," Detective Harrison said with a grunt. "And you didn't simply call the police because...?"

"He damn sure didn't let me grab my cell on the way out. Pay phones disappeared with horse drawn carriages, detective," Charmaine snapped.

"Keep calm," the second detective said quietly.

"So you didn't find Darrius on the street, and you didn't go back to Mrs. Forstall's house," Harrison said.

Charmaine leaned forward and raised her voice. "Hello, murderous thing from hell chewed up a dude! Damn right I didn't go back. Now explain why you guys aren't over there right now."

"The patrol unit got there twenty minutes ago," the second detective said.

"And?"

Detective Harrison and his partner exchanged a glance. Young shook his head before he left the room. "Mrs. Forstall answered the door. She was sleepy and irritated. Says she don't know what you're talking about."

"What? But, but... Search the house. She couldn't have cleaned up blood that fast. You'll find traces and—"

"She wasn't too thrilled about it, but she let the officers take a look around. Not one thing looked out of place. Mrs. Forstall says she fell asleep reading."

"Get forensics to do tests. They'll find DNA from Darrius and Zed. You can search for a match because I know they have felony records for sure. Then we could..." Charmaine's voice trailed off. She blinked rapidly as her thoughts became as tangled as the vines creeping up Mrs. Forstall's trellis.

Detective Harrison planted both his elbows on the table between them. "Look, Charmaine. I don't know what went down last night, but cut it out. You and your sister need to find another game before you get in serious trouble."

"My sister wasn't even with me, and I don't consider bloody murder any kind of game." Charmaine slapped a palm on the table surface. "If you just spent one night in that house, you'd see."

"Mrs. Forstall, not to mention my wife, wouldn't go along with your suggestion. Trust me." Detective Harrison gave a dry laugh.

The door opened and his commander came in with Detective Young behind him. Young gave Harrison a look. Charmaine's psychic skill kicked in. Neither of them had much respect nor liking for the commander, who was new. The commander, well aware he didn't have their field experience, reacted by riding them hard. His ego barely fit inside the small room with the rest of them.

"The detectives filled me in on your colorful statement, Ms. Joliet. Luckily Mrs. Forstall isn't going to press charges," the Commander Murphy said crisply.

Charmaine stood. "Oh hell no! Darrius might be scared, but he needs to be picked up. Of course at the speed he left, the dude might be in Canada by now. Nah, he's got to stick to the city. Y'all got him on lock down."

"Ms. Joliet. Get serious." The commander shook his head at her.

Charmaine gazed at the three faces around the room. Harrison heaved a sigh. Young rubbed his jaw as if thinking.

Commander Murphy stared at her as if he wanted her to disappear.

"Go out and find the man, he's a suspect. She can't refuse to press charges on a murder. Even she doesn't that kind of power or money," Charmaine insisted. "Lucky she didn't press charges on him? What kinda—"

"I meant it's lucky she didn't press charges against you, Ms. Joliet. You admitted going to her house tonight. That's trespassing at the very least, if not breaking and entering."

"Darius had the code, we didn't break in," Charmaine spluttered. "Charge me? I tried to protect the—"

"Then there's criminal mischief and filing a false police report," Commander Murphy went on in a relentless tone. "With the story you cooked up, I wouldn't doubt we could add possession of narcotics or public intoxication. Should we search your car?"

"Search my... what the..." Charmaine fought to gain control and not slap the officious dim-wit. Detective Harrison put a hand on her arm, which distracted her.

"One of our units picked up Darrius James twenty minutes ago. He's not talking. Wants his lawyer. So he's not confirming your story either, Charmaine," Detective Harrison said softly.

"Which wraps up this less than amusing reality show episode," Murphy added. "I've read our files on you, Ms. Joliet. You should avoid drawing attention to yourself, or your sister. You both narrowly escaped felony charges just ten months ago. Not to mention you and Jessi both have a history of mental illness. She hallucinates, and you've been referred to as delusional; think you can see into people's minds."

"Commander, they helped us solve a murder," Harrison put in.

"From what I saw they broke a few laws along the way. Too bad we didn't arrest them," Murphy shot back. "Ms. Joliet, I recommend you and your sister stay clear of police stations from now on. We may not be through with you yet."

Charmaine glared at him. "I'll bet you're not."

"Then you've been warned." Murphy nodded to no one in particular and strode out.

"Jessi had nothing to do with anything. I don't get why y'all keep dragging her name into this." Charmaine turned her ire on Harrison and his partner.

"Because she's given a statement, and she's waiting outside to take you home. Let's go."

Charmaine blinked at him feeling dazed and confused. She followed him out with Detective Young behind her. They went along one hallway, turned left and walked through a busy duty room. Then she passed through locked doors to the lobby. A couple of civilian police employees manned a busy front desk. Police officers came and went. Chairs and three wooden benches lined two walls. Jessi sat chatting with a woman dressed in a tight electric blue jump suit. The woman's eye shadow and blue streaks in her hair matched the jump suit. Jessi stood when she saw Charmaine and the detectives.

"See ya later, Sweet Breezy. Give us a call if you need help. You got our card." Jessi pointed a forefinger at the woman.

"Thanks girl," came the deep throated reply. Sweet Breezy followed Jessi's gaze to Charmaine. "Girl, you gone be alright with your sister on your side."

Jessi strolled over to them. She wore a blood red suede jacket with a fake fur collar. The black pencil skirt hugged her curves, and tall leather boots completed the outfit. "Umph, umph, umph. I can't leave you alone for a minute without you getting into all kinds of mischief. Don't worry detectives. I'll make sure she takes her meds from now on."

"Make sure to take yours while you're at it. We've had enough fun with you two for one night. Hell for a whole month of nights," Detective Young quipped.

"Screw you, too," Jessi retorted and stuck her tongue out at him. She looped an arm through Charmaine's. "Let's go, hunty. I'ma fix you some nice chamomile tea."

"You want to tell me what the hell is going on? We should go back in there and make them listen." Charmaine let Jessi lead her away from the detectives despite her words. Fatigue and nerves weakened her resolve.

"Keep walkin'. I've got to catch you up. And explain my plan," Jessi replied quietly.

6. Something Wicked

Charmaine did indeed accept the offer of tea and sympathy from Jessi. They arrived at Charmaine's bungalow at three o'clock Wednesday morning. Jessi did her duty checking the house. Then she stuck around long enough for Charmaine shower and fill her in. Charmaine described her adventure, yawning through most of it. Then she fell into bed.

Hours later Charmaine woke up from a disturbing dream that she immediately forgot. Only the remnants of a sick feeling of doom and the echoes of screaming still in her head. She sat on the side of her bed for a good twenty minutes to shake it off.

Once dressed, she followed the pulsating base of music coming from the direction of her kitchen. Jessi's best friend Diamond and Charmaine's pal Scotty sat around her kitchen table. Jessi shook her hips to the beat as she stirred something in pot. Diamond grinned encouragement at Charmaine. Scotty, his beefy arms bulging in a dark green sweater, sipped from a cup of hot coffee. An online news site held his attention on the Android tablet propped up in front of him.

"Morning y'all," Charmaine mumbled. She rubbed her forehead to massage away a headache.

"Evening you mean. It's almost four o'clock. C'mon Jessi. I told you to turn off that radio. You woke her up," Scotty spoke loud to the heard over the R&B song.

"I'll do it." Diamond sprang up and turned the volume down low.

"Sis can sleep through a freight train rolling through the house. She ain't no delicate flower. Ain't that right, sis?" Jessi tossed over one shoulder. "I got some of my chicken and sausage gumbo. Oh and some of that low fat spread instead of butter for the French bread. Ugh."

"I read butter is better for you. Most of those spread contain all kinds of artificial stuff." Diamond nodded. "Put some butter out just in case she changes her mind."

"I don't know why you tryin' to lose weight. Guys don't seem to mind your butt, not the way I see 'em lookin'," Jessi quipped.

Scotty put the tablet aside. "Who been lookin'?"

"I'm just sayin'. When Charmaine walks in she gets male attention. Tick tock, girl. If you wanna have some crumb scratchers, get busy. All these men playing hard to get? Blow 'em." Jessi glanced at Diamond with a mischievous grin.

"Humph." Scotty shot Jessi a sideways glance, and then studied Charmaine.

Charmaine ignored him and her sister's annoying attempt to play matchmaker. Scotty and Charmaine had been friends since high school. As grown folks they were friends with benefits. Anything more would complicate a good thing in her opinion. What they had worked. Thankfully Scotty seemed to agree. Mostly. Charmaine did catch him looking at her a little too long every now and then, like he had something on his mind. She dreaded the day he'd decide to have a talk about them. Maybe one day Scotty would get serious about some woman who wanted two kids and a dog. Not Charmaine's speed at all.

"I don't feel like eating." Charmaine dropped into an empty chair at the table. She crossed her arms as if feeling a chill. "We gotta figure out what the hell is going on."

"Harrison probably thinks you're nuts," Jessi joked. When Charmaine shot a nasty look at her, Jessi shrugged. "Hey, join the club. He already knows I'm nuts."

"I don't see how he lives in Louisiana and don't' know spirits are for real," Diamond put in.

"Most of what y'all see turns out to be the living up to no good," Scotty replied.

"You weren't in her house last night. If you'd seen a leg come bouncing from upstairs—" Charmaine inhaled and exhaled a shaky breath.

"You're an expert at reading people, so good it's almost supernatural. No doubt about it."

Jessi turned around, a large spoon in one hand. "Oh, so I'm crazy cause I hear voices and see things."

"I didn't say there ain't unexplained things on this earth. But look at it this way, the Forstall woman is shady. Getting you and Jess involved fits into her game. Let's start there," Scotty said to Charmaine.

"Yeah, maybe." Charmaine leaned back in the chair.

Scotty lifted her legs into his lap. He spoke as he massaged he calves. "I'm telling you the rich can be just as gangsta as anybody in the ghetto. More deadly even."

Jessi raised an eyebrow as she watched his ministrations. She exchanged a knowing look with Diamond, who suppressed a giggle. Charmaine made a note to set them

straight at a later date. They'd been reading those damn romance novels again. She
took her legs from Scotty's lap.

"I just came by to make sure you were
okay. Gotta go open the club. Stay in and
rest your nerves." Scotty rubbed her
shoulders. "I'll call later."

"Sure." Charmaine chewed on a thumb-
nail.

Scotty paused before opening the kitch-
en door. "Do I have to say stay away from
that woman's house? I don't think you
wanna find the rest of whats-his-name."

"Point made," Charmaine blurted out as
she gave a shudder.

"Good. See y'all." Scotty kissed two fingers and held them up to Charmaine before he went through the door.

"We gotta find out more about Mrs. 'lying through her teeth' Forstall," Charmaine said seconds after the door shut.

"Well while you were playing around
with your new pals..." Jessi grinned at the
deadly look Charmaine gave her. "I was actually working the case."

"And?"

"I went snooping, though I don't have a connection in the neighborhood," Jessi said.

"Imagine, you don't have pals working in the Garden District," Charmaine said dryly.

"I'm gone let that one pass," Jessi retorted. "The folks working in those big houses are just as snobby as their employers. I pretended to be waiting for the streetcar. Tried to start a couple of conversations. Nothing."

Diamond leaned forward, arms on the kitchen table. "My great-aunt Orelia worked thirty-five years for one family. Yeah, they pretty loyal."

Jessi brightened. "Maybe your great-aunt will talk to you?"

"She died when I was a kid. Working for the same family was passed down through generations. T-Orelia, that's what we called her, always said she worked all them hours so her daughters could do better."

"Damn, you answered my next question," Jessi said as she dropped into the chair next to Charmaine.

"Sorry." Diamond went to the stove. "This is done. Mind if I take some gumbo home with me? My baby loves gumbo, and so does my brother."

"Sure. I went light on the pepper." Jessi waved a hand.

"What about your ghost boyfriend Lucas?" Charmaine said.

"I waited around until it got dark for nothin'. Lucas acted like I was the police, wouldn't talk. Dude was scared. Freaky, huh?" Jessi frowned.

"A spooked ghost," Diamond said with a laugh "Too funny."

"I tried to find other spirits. When I want peace, they won't shut up. But they decided to play hide and seek yesterday evening. So I went home, probably just a few hours before your boyfriends brought you over for a visit." Jessi tapped Charmaine on the arm.

"The police found Darrius, but he's not cooperating. No big surprise," Charmaine said.

"He had warrants out on him, so he'll be in jail for awhile," Jessi said.

"You've been busy. Hope you're not tired because we've got more research to do." Charmaine looked at her.

"Then we go back to visit Mrs. Got Bucks?" Jessi sat straight, eyes gleaming.

"Damn right," Charmaine replied.

"But Scotty said you should rest, and stay away from the place." Diamond started to go on, but she stopped at the look the sisters gave her.

Charmaine stood. "I decide where I go and what I do."

7. Loose Ends

At nine o'clock the next night, Charmaine and Jessi parked a black Jeep Grand Cherokee one street over from the Forstall mansion. A five minute walk to the small private street would take them there. Jessi had rented the Jeep figuring Charmaine's car might be recognized. They sipped mocha lattes. Jessi blew smoke from a slender cigar through a crack in the window.

"Thought you quit," Charmaine said as she continued to scroll through notes on her tablet computer.

"We're about to face some serious supernatural shit. I need a drink and one of those big Cubans instead of this little thing." Jessi took another puff.

"Me, too, but no drinking. We gotta be sharp for this one."

"Okay, Mr. Forstall isn't in Italy. So where is he?" Charmaine glanced down the narrow street. She could just see the northern corner of Mrs. Forstall's house.

"According to Alyssa, the daughter, he went to his French mistress instead. Somewhere in the southern part of France. She wasn't sure where." Jessi stared at her cell phone.

"Bless you Instagram, Snapchat, and over-sharing teenagers. So maybe the son knows?" Charmaine glanced up from her tablet.

"He doesn't give a crap about the old man. He told Alyssa to be happy the 'lying ho sperm donor' got out of her life while she young," Jessi said with a snort. She continued to scan her social accounts on the cell phone. "Dang, think of all the great stuff we could have done back in the day with these apps."

"Yeah, get into even bigger trouble," Charmaine retorted.

"Like I said, it would have been beyond cool," Jessi quipped.

"Daddy Forstall isn't in France any more than he is in Italy. Mama Forstall has secrets as we well know from Darrius." Charmaine tapped her fingers on the steering wheel.

"Blackmail worthy secrets. So you think..." Jessi glanced at Charmaine sideways.

"What if her husband found out or was on the verge of uncovering said nasty secrets? He could still be in the house."

Jessi sat silently for a few beats. Then she shook her head. "Some of these rich couples lead separate lives. He's doing his thang and she's doing hers. Nah, I don't think he'd care. But they will get lethal when it comes to their money."

"Neither one of the kids could be his. That's a game changer. No inheritance for them or her. But you can't just get rid of a husband these days. Somebody would put it together." Charmaine frowned into the darkness.

"Or he could be with the French mistress after all. The son might know," Jessi replied. She put her cell phone in an inner jacket pocket and zipped it.

"Yeah, get his preferred social media handle and ask."

"Screw this. Let's ask her." Jessi glanced around. "She should be having an after dinner drink right about now. We can catch her off guard."

"Or we could wait a few more days and get more info," Charmaine countered. "No rush."

"And what will change? Harrison won't budge on a missing husband. Not when he finds out the guy has two mistresses. We got paid, right?"

"The check went through and is in our biz account," Charmaine said. "But I doubt Mrs. Forstall will pay us that big final payment for ridding the house of her ghost, ghoul or whatever the heck that thing is."

"Hell no. We'll figure out what's going on and give her incentive to pay up or else," Jessi said.

"Umm, that's called extortion and it's illegal. All she has to do is call Harrison. We'll be wearing matching prison uniforms. Forget it."

"Yeah, but—"

"Did I stutter? We're not going to hand her ammunition to use against us."

"Can't have no fun with you," Jessi muttered.

"Whatever. Now let me get situated before we go in the house. Smart to get this tricked out Jeep. We blend in with the rest of these fancy SUVs."

Charmaine checked the bag she would carry instead of a purse. She'd packed four small bundles of dried white sage and cedar. She'd burn them outside the house to weaken any spirits, making them less dangerous. She had three bottles of colloidal silver in liquid form and salt. Finally the heavy artillery, a cross and six tiny spray bottles of holy water.

"Stop with that hocus-pocus mess. I packed something useful." Jessi held up two objects.

"A gun and a taser. You want to get us arrested, huh?" Charmaine heaved a deep sigh.

"Not just any gun and not just any old taser. First, I've got actual silver bullets in this bad girl." Jessi kissed the small semi-automatic pistol. She stuck it back into a jacket pocket.

"Great in case we run into a werewolf," Charmaine replied. "What's that other thingamabob?"

"Spirits are matter, well subatomic particles. I read up on the history of psychic scientific research. An electrical charge will disrupt the particles, sorta like kicking a ghost in the nuts." Jessi grinned.

"Let's hope the thing is a guy," Charmaine clipped.

"Hey, I got science, not superstition. While you wave burning leaves, I'll take the thing out." Jessi gave a sharp nod. She stuck the device into a holster clipped to her waist. "I'm ready for his ghostly ass. Let's go."

Charmaine got out of the Jeep and waited as Jessi came around from the passenger side to join her. "I'm ready only because Mrs. Forstall is alone, except for a troll or whatever it is."

"Darrius killed Zed and put on a show just for you. Maybe those two cooked it up," Jessi said quietly. She scanned their surroundings.

"He never went upstairs. Judging by the way he reacted, I'd say he wasn't in on it. This way."

Charmaine nodded as she shined a flashlight on the ground. The small paved alley, called Jasmine Lane, was just wide enough for one vehicle. Tall shrubs bordered either side of it. The lane widened several yards in to allow two vehicles to pass, then narrowed again.

"He could have been acting. Darrius ran up the stairs, killed Zed and got back down. Those sounds had you freaking out, too. Mrs. Forstall was chattering away about being scared. Think about it," Jessi whispered even though no one seemed around.

"Okay, say I looked away. That gruesome racket upstairs did rattle me, no lie. But Darrius would have had to be superhuman to move so fast," Charmaine whispered back.

She walked several feet before she realized Jessi had vanished. Her heart did several back flips as she gazed into shadows. Charmaine called her name in a low raspy voice. Rising panic fought with her need to keep Mrs. Forstall or the neighbors from hearing them. Then her flashlight winked off.

"Damn it."

Charmaine struggled to keep her imagination from seeing menacing figures everywhere. A row of boxwood hedges marked the border of the property next door. A darker shape to her left moved. Charmaine raced forward only to get scratched by a large holly bush.

"Owee, damn," she hissed.

"Keep quiet. You want the entire Garden District to come out here shooting?" Jessi said quietly.

"What the—"

"I'm fine. Lucas showed up and wanted to talk. He apologized for the way he acted the other night." Jessi grabbed Charmaine's right arm to steady her.

"Make up with your ghost boyfriend some other time. I don't want to be in that house too late at night." Charmaine glanced at the mansion. There was one lighted window on the second floor. The first floor seemed more lit up.

Jessi pulled Charmaine into an opening. A stone bench faced a small bird bath. "You want to hear what Lucas told me. The Forstall how has a couple of nasty spirits. Unpleasant is how he put it. But the real scary thing chased them off. Lucas says evil in the family has growing for over one hundred years."

Charmaine forgot to be annoyed as she sat down hard on the bench. "Fits with the family history I found. One ancestor made his money in the slave trade. Another tortured a series of mistresses. There were rumors he killed a few. But I've never heard of evil turning into an entity."

"Maybe it's like static electricity. With the right conditions friction creates energy, static electricity that can cause pain. Could be the 'thing' has had enough time to move on its own," Jessie said with a frown.

"And become deadly. Damn, you're starting to make sense," Charmaine murmured.

"Lucas is glad they sent the kids away. Lucas hates these folks after the life he had, so if he's relieved..." Jessi's voice trailed off as she looked toward the Forstall mansion.

"Then it's bad," Charmaine said.

"Exactly." Jessi stopped talking suddenly. "Hold up. I see two people looks like. Come on."

Jessi yanked Charmaine to her feet. She ran at a crouch across the back lawn, with Charmaine being dragged along. She finally jerked free from Jessi's grasp as they got close to the house. Silhouettes against the expensive draperies did indeed show one taller and a shorter figure. Charmaine and Jessi looked at each other and then at the window again.

"Who?" Charmaine mouthed.

"Let's find out," Jessi whispered back.

Before Charmaine could stop her, Jessi disappeared around the corner of the house. Charmaine cringed at the faint crunch of her sister's footsteps on the gravel drive way. She fought to control her breathing from their sprint across the wide lawn. Then she followed Jessi's presumed path down the side of the house. She kept low and close to the outer wall. Then Charmaine froze at the muted sound of voices. A thick arm wrapped around her body pinning both arms to her side. Her feet flew off the ground. Wet lips pressed against Charmaine's left ear lope.

"Come join the party, bitch," a familiar voice said. "Don't disturb the good neighbors if you care about your little sis."

8. Triple Cross

Charmaine tried and failed not to visibly tremble when Darrius dragged her inside. They retraced their steps from the fateful night Zed met his end. She would have screamed or at least whimpered, but Charmaine had trouble breathing. The big man's tight grip didn't help. He shoved her hard into the library, which caused her to fall. Quick reflexes saved Charmaine from landing face down. Instead she remembered her gym days at school and caught herself, both palms flat on the Persian wool carpet. She looked up to find Mrs. Forstall holding a gun on Jessi.

"Much as I like a woman on her knees..." Darrius licked his bottom lip. "Get up and stand over there next to your sister."

Mrs. Forstall stepped away from Jessi. "Do as you're told."

"I just thought of something. The psychics didn't see this one comin'." Darrius snickered at his own joke.

Loretta smiled. "Good one."

Jessi beat Charmaine to the burning question. "Your triflin' ass supposed to be in jail."

Darrius took an automatic pistol from the back waistband of his jeans. He struck a relaxed pose against Mr. Forstall's massive desk. "The police didn't have enough to charge me with murder. I got bonded out on them other little charges."

"Who...?" Charmaine glanced at Mrs. Forstall.

"We have mutual interests," Mrs. Forstall replied mildly.

"Yeah, we sure as hell do. Loretta figured out helping me was in her best interest." Darrius winked at the sisters.

Charmaine twitched at the powerful desire to punch the smug grin from his face. "Dude, you can't trust her."

"I can't trust anybody in this world. But I got insurance." Darrius held the gun loosely without pointing it at them.

"I've got them under control. Go up and get your share of the gold coins from the safe. It's open." Mrs. Forstall smiled as she gave him a quick sideways glance.

"That's what I'm talkin' about," Darrius replied.

"Aren't you worried about meeting that people eater? Think what happened to your friend," Charmaine darted a fearful glance at the ceiling.

Darrius and Mrs. Forstall laughed, but he spoke. "C'mon, you really fell for that bullshit. Ain't no monster up there."

"Damn, you killed your friend. You're right. The monster is down here," Jessi said. Her expression hardened.

"Zed and me did business a few times, but he wasn't my friend. I told him about this job, and he jumped at the chance." Darrius laughed.

"You set up the poor fool," Charmaine spat at him.

"Zed wasn't was a stone cold killer, a thief and he liked little girls. I did the world a favor the way I see it. Sick fuck."

"Oh sure. You're a damn hero cleaning up the streets of New Orleans. Now I see the cape," Jessi said with a snort.

"Hey, I kinda like that." Darrius smiled nastily. "Call me Street Sweeper."

"I can think of a few other things to call you." Jessi hissed and started to illustrate, but Charmaine held up a hand. She stopped but glared at Darrius.

"You didn't have time to go up stairs and kill him. I was looking at you the whole time," Charmaine said.

"Loretta set a booby trap with sharp blades. That noise you heard? That was gears working when Zed opened the closet door where the safe is. Whoosh, screech, and bye-bye gangsta." Darrius waved a hand then snickered.

"Quite an ingenious tool left by one of my ancestors. We found it when we cleared out the attic for renovations fifteen years ago. The thing has no practical use except getting rid of inconvenient people. Apparently the whispers about my great-great grandfather were true." Mrs. Forstall shrugged. "Oh well, everyone has a few crooked branches in their family tree."

"Some have more than few," Jessi mumbled.

"You kept a killing machine because you thought it might come in handy?" Charmaine gazed at her in morbid fascination.

"And it did. Enough talk. Let's get moving. I have a plane to catch." Mrs. Forstall cast a sideways glance at Darrius and nodded for him to leave.

"Look, I don't know what she promised you, but I think you need a new business partner," Charmaine said.

"I got a lot less to lose. I ain't no socialite with a fancy name and reputation to protect," Darrius replied.

"He's right of course, which is why he'll be joining you in the great beyond," Mrs. Forstall said.

A tall man with salt and pepper hair appeared from a sliding panel in the wall.

The revolver he pointed looked more lethal than the automatic pistol Darrius had.
He wore a cashmere wool blend jacket,
pale blue shirt and navy blue slacks. His
leather shoes alone probably cost more
than three of Charmaine's car notes. He
could have stepped from the pages of St.
Charles Ave., a glossy magazine about the
city's wealthy class.

Darrius stood rigid. His eyes glittered as
he aimed at the newcomer's head. "What
the hell is goin' on?"

"You may notice the resemblance to this
portrait of his grandfather," Mrs. Forstall
gestured to a painting over the fireplace.
"But I won't keep you in suspense. Meet
my handsome husband, Hamilton Bienville
Forstall."

"You're an attractive bunch. I wish we
could have met under better circumstanc-
es. As it is, we'll have to kill you all," her
husband drawled in a cultured tone. He
might have been expressing regrets that a
dinner party had been cancelled.

"I don't think so, slick. I've got a gun,
too," Darrius growled. "So drop it or I'll

plug the missus and then you. And then the whole world gonna know you been stealin' from the family company, and they'll get video of our sex games."

"Think carefully, dear. Who gave you the gun?" Mrs. Forstall raised a perfectly arched auburn eyebrow.

Hamilton Forstall shook his head, and then laughed. "You told me, but I didn't believe he was that dumb."

Darrius pulled the trigger several times. "You lyin' bitch."

"Watching my wife screw you this way is even more fun," Hamilton Forstall said.

He ducked when Darrius threw the gun at him. Darrius let loose with a stream of profanity. He included ever generation of both sides of their families. Then he started in on the rest of the world. Jessi exchanged a glance with Charmaine, a message in her dark gaze. Maybe they could take advantage of the distraction. Charmaine lifted her head just enough to signal she understood.

"I don't get why you hired us?" Charmaine gazed at Hamilton Forstall to keep him from paying attention to Jessi.

"We needed witnesses to verify Shawntelle tried to blackmail us, and Darrius had a motive to kill her," he replied in a cool voice.

"We certainly couldn't go to our society friends for help, could we?" his wife added. "Besides, she did in fact blackmail us. Both of them did. They're greedy, always demanding more and more."

"So there's no ghost," Charmaine said.

"Oh, that old thing. It's been bumping around for generations. Mostly moving a candle stick a few inches, making the usual noises an old house makes even louder. Nothing serious. But the stories are legend, so we capitalized on it." Mrs. Forstall gave a casual shrug.

"You knew we'd research your family and find the stories," Jessi put in.

Mrs. Forstall nodded. "Credibility."

Hamilton Forstall's smile twisted into something terrible. "Darrius enjoyed the feeling of power he had to destroy us. He and Shawntelle didn't just want money. They wanted to own us. They used our vacation home whenever they wanted. Trashed the place. He even forced me into letting him drive my father's vintage 1948 Bentley. Can you imagine? A classic parked at some crack house in the ninth ward? Intolerable."

"Simply killing them had its disadvantages, so we got creative. Ham thought of using my ancestor's little contraption as a prop. Brilliant, dear," Mrs. Forstall said.

"Thanks, darling."

"A prop? You used it to murder a man," Charmaine shot back, giving them the deadly couple a scowl.

"Actually I killed the thug. Cutting off one of his legs was an added bit of drama." Hamilton lifted his chin.

"They're going to kill us and leave town," Jessi said to Charmaine. Then she looked at the Forstalls. "The story is going to be Darrius came back here to steal and get revenge. We confronted him because we were here for the same reason. He killed us, but we managed to shoot him during the fight. He dies from his wounds."

"You truly are psychic darling," Mrs. Forstall said with a smile.

"They're not only pretty, but quite smart. Too bad we can't enjoy them before..." Hamilton studied Jessi and then Charmaine, a sparkle of lust in his hazel eyes.

"No time sweetheart. Your fingerprints and DNA are all over the house. Our house cleaners will verify we left town. They'll find your bodies in the morning. Darrius will be discovered in an alley some miles away. Evidence will show he bled to death from his wounds."

"Neighbors will hear the shots," Charmaine said.

"We love our privacy. The house has sound absorbing wall paper. We even managed to comply with local historical reservation ordinances." Mrs. Forstall smiled with pride.

"So it seems like y'all thought of everything. Almost," Jessi said.

Her eyes went glassy. She swayed as if about the faint. Charmaine put an arm around her shoulder and braced herself. The lights flickered, but stopped after ten seconds.

"Damn it, we should sue that electrical contractor, Loretta," Hamilton growled in irritation.

"You muthafuckas ain't gonna take me out," Darrius blurted when the lights flickered a second time.

The lights inside the house went out. Then yard lamp bulbs outside shattered. Jessi started to hum low in her throat. Mr. and Mrs. Forstall cursed when running feet pounded toward the door. A second set of rapid thumps followed. Charmaine pulled a limp Jessi down to the floor seconds before a gun went off. She bumped up against the desk and used it as a shield. She hoped darkness and panic would throw off Mrs. Forstall.

"You little ghetto rats better stay put. I'll kill you now rather than later," Mrs. Forstall called out, her voice high-pitched with terror. "Makes no difference to me."

"Get away. Get away!" Hamilton Forstall shouted from somewhere in the house.

"He's upstairs," Jessi mumbled.

"Ham? Ham, answer me. This is no time to play ghost games," Mrs. Forstall shouted. "Hamilton!"

"Get it off me," Darrius screamed from another direction deep in the house.

Then it started; the heavy thump, thump of a dense object dragging across the floor. Grinding noises, a cross between groaning and wheezing breaths surrounded them. The sound became palpable, making the darkness thicker. The atmosphere around them pressed in as if a humid fog filled the room. Crunching. More screams tore through the air. More shots. The house shuddered.

"We better get out. Out," Jessi yelled.

She thrashed around in Charmaine's arms until she stood. Charmaine jumped to her feet and gripped Jessi's hand. Using touch and memory only, Charmaine dashed to the French doors. One kick, then another. Wood and glass gave way. The awful sound of human wails and grinding chased them into the night. Sirens added to the pandemonium. And they kept running.

****

Three hours later Charmaine and Jessi sat in the back seat of Detective Harrison's unmarked Chevy Malibu. They both shivered, but not because of the chilly temperatures. Musty police issue blankets helped anchor them to a more mundane world. For once the flash of police lights comforted them. NOPD uniforms moved around securing the crime scene. Techs suited up to enter the house. Harrison crisply issued order, fully in control. Finally he walked over to the car. Harrison rubbed a hand roughly over his close cut hair. He sighed several times then leaned on the car, one hand on the hood bracing him.

"Let me get this straight. The Forstalls engineered the entire scheme because they were being blackmailed. So they killed three people," Harrison huffed out.

"Hamilton Forstall fought his two older brothers for years over control of the business. He filed two lawsuits," Charmaine said. "It's all online. I found four articles written back in the nineties. He lost in 2008. Stealing from the company was his revenge."

"Plus they didn't want their reputations to go south. Imagine sex tapes of them on the internet for eternity. When you find Darrius's phone, you'll probably find them. Check if he has a desktop or tablet computer, too." Jessi sound weak. She yawned, closed her eyes and rested her head on the back of the car seat.

"Yeah, but gunshots don't explain the bloody mess in there. Three dead people, two of them among the most prominent New Orleans citizens. Jesus, what a nightmare," Harrison nodded at the house. "Looks like something out of a horror movie. You two wanna explain? Wait a minute, don't answer. I'm guessing it's nothing I can put in an official report that won't get me fired and committed to a psych ward."

"Okay, they started arguing about the blackmail. Things got out of hand and everybody started shooting. Mr. Forstall used that antique torture tool to hack up Darrius. In the dark everybody got slashed, shot and dead." Jessi spoke without opening her eyes.

Charmaine looked up at Harrison. "We'll back up they were all nut jobs with a taste for violence. I mean they tried to kill us."

Harrison stood straight with another deep sigh, followed by a grunt. "I'll make it work. Great. The pimple on my ass shows."

His commander sat in a police Tahoe for a few minutes talking on the phone. He scanned the area, found Harrison and beckoned him with a sharp hand movement. With another grunt of resignation, Harrison trudged off in Murphy's direction.

"Now we can talk the real deal. Lucas?" Charmaine gazed into the night as if she could see him.

"Yeah, plus he brought reinforcements. He was too scared to come alone," Jessi mumbled.

"Your ghost boyfriend to the rescue," Charmaine teased.

"He ain't my boyfriend, and he's too jumpy for my taste."

"You almost passed out. What was that about?"

Jessi sat up, eyes open. "Lucas and the others started all talking at once. But I got the gist. I reached out to the... not sure what to call it. Negative force I guess. What about the lights? Sure wasn't me."

"I started thinking how we needed to get away. I stared at the lights, blocked out everything else and prayed hard. Then they flickered and went out. Didn't know I could direct objects. Thank you, Lord."

"There you go with the God nonsense. Pure energy and you've been practicing control of it. Remember? Science, not superstition," Jessi countered.

"Intelligent design. Even Einstein said so. God is real, Jess."

Jessi led her head fall back and closed her eyes. "Whatev. I'm too worn out to argue with you."

"We gotta deal with that thing in the house. Alyssa and Grayson will be in danger," Charmaine said as she gazed at the Forstall mansion.

"Agreed, though I doubt they'll want to live there ever again. My bet is they sell the place. Still, we can't let a string of rich white folks end up as ghost snacks. Wouldn't be very polite," Jessi murmured, her words slurred by fatigue.

"I don't see how you can sleep. I won't for a long time. That awful sound keeps echoing in my head, even through all the chaos. Staying awake looks really good to me now. I want some normal back in my life for a minute. Hey, I feel like Belgian waffles. What about you?"

Jessi's soft snoring was the only answer she got.

About the Author

Mix knowledge of voodoo, Louisiana politics and forensic social work with the dedication to write fiction while working each day as a clinical social worker, and you get a snapshot of author Lynn Emery. Lynn has been a contributing consultant to the magazine *Today's Black Woman* for three articles about contemporary relationships between black men and women. For more information visit: www.lynnemery.com

CPSIA information can be obtained
at www.ICGtesting.com
Printed in the USA
LVHW11s1431071018
592735LV00002B/376/P

9 780996 527279